NO WAY HOME

L.A. DAVENPORT

P-WAVE
PRESS

P-Wave Press

Cover design by David Löwe

p-wavepress.co.uk

A CIP catalogue record for this book is available from the British Library.

ISBN 9781999595784

eISBN 9781999595746

CONTENTS

Screen Grab   1

The White Room   43

Deathcast   57

Cut Out and Keep   133

Stations of the Soul   149

The Lake   225

About the Author   235
By L.A. Davenport   237
P-Wave Press   239

SCREEN GRAB

Thanks to A— for the title

I

REFLECTED IN A DUSTY COMPUTER SCREEN IS A MESSY bedroom, strewn with long-discarded toys, cheap clothes, half-read magazines, unread books and all the detritus of a young life. The room is silent, still, waiting.

A nearby door opens and slams shut, and feet tip-tap their way towards the bedroom.

"Is that you, Lauren?" a voice calls from another room. The footsteps stop.

"Yes, mum."

The steps, slower and quieter now, continue down the hall. In the reflection of the dusty screen, the door opens and Lauren slouches in, throwing her bag on the unmade bed. Without looking around, she walks straight over to the screen, sits down and turns on the computer.

"Dinner's ready in five," the voice calls from another room.

Lauren watches the computer slowly start up.

"D'you hear me?"

Lauren bites her fingernails and jiggles her foot up and down.

"Oi, madam. Are you listening to me? Dinner. Five minutes."

Lauren looks at the door. "Yeah, I got it," she shouts back. She turns back to the computer screen. "I can hear you, you drunk bitch," she whispers.

The computer fan speeds up and Lauren roots through her bag while she waits. Eventually, the computer finishes loading, and Lauren opens a teenage website, full of selfies, photos of food, links to articles, YouTube videos, adverts and celebrity endorsements. Ignoring everything else on the screen, Lauren navigates straight to the chatrooms, where an endless stream of scrolling messages loads, one after another after another. She watches the hellos, the ongoing chats, the comments and the complaints pass by. She then selects a particular chat room and enters. The conversation scrolls quickly up the screen, joined at the end by an automated message:

L-KAT has entered the room.

Lauren types.
L-KAT: hi evry1. How r u?

A string of greetings flows up the screen, welcoming L-KAT into the room, asking her about school and how home is today. One user asks her whether her mum is paying her any attention.

L-KAT: hey, yeh, im okay. scool okay. Skved home, but no hassl. No-1 noticed…Mumz drunk again.

A message flashes across the centre of the screen:

Private chat request from gTV
Accept | Decline

Lauren moves her mouse and clicks 'Accept'. A new,

private chat window opens, with a cursor flashing in the corner, waiting.

The voice in the other room calls: "Dinner's ready."

"Okay."

A message appears in the blank window.

gTV: Hello Lauren. How are you?

L-KAT: alrite. U?

gTV: I'm fine, thank you. How was school today?

L-KAT: ok. shit. bt ok.

gTV: I'm sorry to hear that, Lauren. And your mum? How is she today?

The voice shouts: "Come on Lauren. Get off that bloody computer and have your dinner before it gets cold."

"Coming," Lauren shouts back.

L-KAT: Shes bein a bitch.

gTV: Don't worry, Lauren. You aren't alone. You can talk to me anytime you know.

L-KAT: Thx appreci8 it. u herd anyting?

gTV: Yes, I have. It's definitely all going ahead. I'll know the exact date soon. It's all just between us, though, okay? You can't tell anyone.

L-KAT: Course.

The voice bursts into the room and Lauren's mum stands in the doorway, waving a wooden spoon. "Get off that computer now, Lauren, and come and eat your bloody dinner."

Lauren turns off the computer screen. "All right, all right."

II

A COTTAGE, RAMSHACKLE AND DILAPIDATED, SQUATS uncomfortably in the middle of a copse. The damp fog of early autumn permeates everything, pushing through the crumbling walls and rotting window frames, slowly engulfing the decaying pile of bricks. Aside from occasional dripping of water from the trees, all is silent and still.

Inside, the hall is dank and cold. The thin, grey light barely pushes through the dirty glass panes, and the corners are hung with mysterious shadows. Mould and moss grow up the walls and the wallpaper and plaster are peeling. A stained and threadbare rug lies in the middle of the floor. A small chandelier, dirty and forgotten, hangs from the ceiling. On one side, a large staircase, with several collapsed steps, climbs unsteadily up to the first floor. Opposite sits a large fireplace that has clearly not been touched in years.

The front door swings open and slams against the wall.

The room settles back into silence.

Minutes later, a tall, thin man with greasy hair and a beard and dressed in shabby clothes, steps onto the threshold. He stands, listening, taking in his surroundings. Satisfied he is alone, he steps fully into the cottage, throws down a rucksack and looks around. After a moment of contemplation, he steps takes a further step into middle of the hall. Tentatively, with his ear lifted into the decaying space all around him, the man listens to the house.

Nothing.

Opening the door on the opposite side of the hall, he steps into a dilapidated kitchen. The sink is dirty and full of broken plates. The cupboard doors are hanging off their hinges, revealing bare, dusty shelves. Mould is growing on the window panes. The backdoor to the clearing behind the house looks as if it hasn't been opened in years. The man runs his hand over a large table in the middle of the room. He steps over an upended, broken chair. He tries a tap. The pipes gurgle and a thin ribbon of brown water trickles out. He places his hands on the edge of the sink and contemplates the view out of the window. Pushing himself upright, he straightens a chair, closes a drawer and places the lid back on a blackened and dirty teapot. He walks over to the back door and, after trying the handle several times, shoves it open with his shoulder. The slow drip-drip in the copse invades the dead air of the forgotten room. He watches a leaf fall from a tree.

The man steps out into the clearing. It must have been a garden once, divided off from the rest by a low stone wall, now almost reclaimed by the slow encroachment of nature. He spots an old washing line slung between the house and a nearby tree. The cord is damp and rough in his hands. Garden tools lie abandoned in the weeds and long grass.

He places his hands on his hips and thinks, and then walks back into the kitchen.

Back inside, he spots another door in the corner of the room, finding another set of stairs. He climbs slowly, exploring each step as he goes. Halfway up, a plank squeaks loudly and he stops, listening carefully. Satisfied there is no one, he rocks his foot back and forth on the step, examining how the sound is made, before continuing up the stairs.

At the top, he finds a small landing with a door. He waits, listening, frowning, with his head cocked to one side. He tries the door and finds a corridor lined with doors, leading, at the end, back to the main stairs and the hall below. He opens each door in turn, poking his head around and then moving onto the next. At the end, he walks slowly down the main stairs, stopping at the bottom step and looking around. Noticing he had left the front door open, he gently pushes it shut. He turns back to the hall, leaning on the front door and taking in his surroundings. He contemplates the fireplace and an old, worn armchair beside it. He breathes in the dank, heavy air and sighs.

Back in the kitchen, he finds a chair that isn't broken and sits down, placing his feet on the table. All is silent, aside from the chirruping of a bird in the trees outside the window. The man runs a hand through his beard and smiles.

III

A CONSTANT STREAM OF MESSAGES SCROLLS UP THE COMPUTER screen in Lauren's bedroom. Users join and leave the chat room, greet each other, ask questions, make comments. On the list of inactive members is g-TV. A nearby door opens and slams shut and feet tip-tap their way towards the bedroom.

"Where do you think you're going," a voice calls out from another room. The footsteps stop. "Get in here."

"I just wanted to…"

"Now," the voice shouts angrily.

Slowly, the steps lead away from the bedroom. All the while, messages scroll endlessly up the screen, and the computer's hard drive clicks and whirs.

"Sit down," the voice says in the other room. "I said sit down."

The messages continue to scroll.

"Do you know what happened today," the voice demands. "Hey, don't sit there staring at your fucking trainers, young lady. I asked you a fucking question. Do you know what happened today?"

"No," Lauren says quietly.

"I got a call from the school."

The clicking and whirring of the computer hard drive continues.

"Do you know what they said," the voice asked. "Do you what they said?" she shouted.

"No."

"Well, you bloody well should do. They said you weren't at school. They said you missed some lessons. English and something else, I don't know what. Well? What have you got to say for yourself?"

The messages continue scrolling, and three people join the chat room.

"So you've got nothing to say?" the voice bellows. "Nothing at all? You cocky little madam. Who the fuck do you think you are? And after all I do for you."

There is a scuffle and then a slap. Lauren squeals and runs down the corridor. Reflected in the screen, the bedroom door swings open and Lauren bursts in, throwing down her bag and slamming the door shut. Without taking her coat off, she slumps into the chair and stares emptily at the messages scrolling on and on up the screen. Tears begin to roll down her cheeks and she sobs.

Eventually, she stops crying and stares at the desk. Out of the corner of her eye, she sees the scrolling messages of the chat room and turns towards the computer screen. She types on the keyboard and a message flashes up:

L-KAT has entered the room.

She types again and a message appears at the bottom of the screen.

L-KAT: hi evry1. How r u?

Greetings flow up the screen, one after another

welcoming L-KAT. Several people ask about her mum and how school was today.

Lauren types.

L-KAT: Bad. An mum hates me.

gTV moves from the inactive to the active user list.

A few more messages appear in the chat room window, and then a message flashes across the centre of the screen:

Private chat request from gTV
Accept | Decline

Lauren clicks 'Accept' and a new chat window opens, with the cursor flashing in the corner, waiting. 'gTV is typing' the window notes.

gTV: How are you today, Lauren?

L-KAT: Bad. U?

gTV: I'm fine, thank you. What's happened?

L-KAT: Mums horrible.

gTV: I'm sorry to hear that, Lauren. I can understand how you feel. What did she say this time?

L-KAT: She say 'm cocky an slapped me.

gTV: I'm sorry. You deserve better than that, Lauren.

L-KAT: Yeah, 2 rite. R we still on 4 tomorro?

gTV: Yes, absolutely, it's all set. Are you ready, Lauren?

L-KAT: Yep.

gTV: So you'll be there at 7am?

L-KAT: Yep.

gTV: Make you sure you don't wake your mum when you leave.

L-KAT: No. She wont hear nuthin. Shell still b drunk. Sheez neva up b4 10.

gTV: Promise you'll be there at 7am, Lauren. Otherwise I'll have to go without you and you won't get to meet him.

L-KAT: Ill b ther. An he better b there 2. I want 2 meet him.

The screen is static. Lauren types, frowning at the screen.

L-KAT: U promise?

Nothing.

L-KAT: U ther?

After what seems like an eternity, 'gTV is typing' appears in the window.

gTV: Yes, Lauren. He will be there, but only as long as you are. But you can't tell anyone anything about this. No-one. It has to be our secret for now. You can tell people about it afterwards, but not before. Okay? Do you understand?

L-KAT: Course. We agree alredy. I aint stupid.

gTV: And make sure to remember to wear the top we talked about, so I'll know that it's you.

Lauren's mother bursts into the room. "Did I tell you you could use that fucking computer? Turn it off. NOW."

The screen goes black and the messages disappear.

IV

The tall, bearded man tramps across a ploughed field towards the copse. He carries a large canvas bag stuffed full of vegetables, with a bundle of sticks tucked under one arm and a box of eggs under the other. The cold air hangs thick and heavy, and mist obscures the world beyond the trees. A car passes on a narrow country lane, hidden from view by a thick, ancient hedge.

Inside the copse, the man steps over the fallen branches and wet leaves, but can't stop his long, torn trousers from becoming damp halfway up to his knees. The windows of the cottage, dead eyes in a pockmarked face, stare blankly at him as he approaches.

He walks straight up to the front door and kicks it open, hooking it shut again with his foot once he is inside. Inside, the cottage is tidy. The rug is gone and the floor has been swept of leaves and mouse droppings. Everything has been dusted and there are the faint hints of former glories in the scrubbed sheen of what remains of the plasterwork. The man drops the bundle of sticks by the fireside and walks into the kitchen, carefully plucking the box of eggs from underneath his arm and placing the bag of shopping on the kitchen table. He unpacks the bag, sorting through the vegetables and placing those that need washing in the now-empty and clean sink. The rest he puts into the cupboards, now dusted and washed, with their doors repaired. He then places a saucepan of water on a small camp stove next to the sink and lights it before heading out the back door and into the garden, where he checks his washing, strung out along the line. He unpegs a sheet and a blanket and some of his clothes and bundles them up under his arm. He takes them into the hall and dumps them in a chair opposite the fireplace, and then busies himself with starting a fire made from the sticks and some logs piled up next to the grate. Once the fire has taken, he sets out his washing on the backs of chairs all around the hall and over the doors, and admires his handiwork.

Remembering something, he fishes around in a pocket and pulls out a tatty picture of a younger, cleaner man with a young girl. He gazes at the picture for a while before placing it behind a candlestick on the mantelpiece. He straightens out a corner of the picture, lingers for a moment, and then climbs the stairs, careful to avoid the missing steps. Overcome with tiredness, he walks slowly along the landing and enters one of the rooms. It has a sloping roof and bare walls, with wooden laths showing through holes in the peeling wallpaper. There is a stained and lumpy unmade bed in the middle of one wall, with a decaying chest of drawers on one side. A tired old wardrobe stands in one corner.

The man's footsteps on the old, solid floorboards creak as he walks over to the bed. He stands next to it for a while, gazing absentmindedly out of the skylight at the treetops and the mist. As he undoes his old and frayed shirt he is interrupted by scratching on the roof. He steps over to the window and inches it open. Two pigeons fly past and the man watches them skirt the trees and disappear. He gazes down onto the clearing, then into the copse and the field beyond. He notices for the first time a path through the trees from the road, and wonders about the last time someone drove along it. Maybe not so long ago, judging by the tracks and the lack of plant growth. He stares out into the grey mist. A pick-up trundle past on the road. He closes the window and turns back towards the bed, slowly pulling open the rest of his shirt buttons.

HOURS LATER, he walks slowly down the stairs, lost in thought. At the bottom step, he stands and looks around, spotting a door he realises he's never opened. Frowning, he walks over and shoves it open. The room is dark and the threadbare curtains have clearly not been opened for a long time. The air is heavy with dust and there is a strange smell. As his eyes adjust to the light, he notices a large sofa along one wall, with a bookcase next to it, a dresser dotted with long-forgotten knick-knacks on the opposite wall and a broken cane chair. In the middle of the room lies an old and heavily stained rug. The man spots a gap between the sofa and the wall. He walks over and leans over the sofa. He frowns and looks a little more closely. In the shadows lies a blue hold-all that looks almost new.

He pulls back the sofa and kneels down, tugging at the zip. Shocked, he pulls out ropes, handcuffs, restraints, knives and a pair of pliers. At the bottom, he finds a saw and a blood-stained hammer. The man falls back against the wall, staring in disbelief, his heart pounding. He looks up and stares at the dresser. Pointing straight at him is a video camera.

He pulls himself up and walks over to the camera, inspecting it as best as he can without touching it. A red light is flashing on the back. He tries to work out what the symbols on the camera mean, eventually turning it around so that he can get a proper look. He presses a button and the camera starts into life. The man steps back in surprise, and then notices that the camera has a fold-out display. He tentatively pulls it out. The screen indicates that two hours of video have been recorded. He hesitates and then presses 'Play'.

The video crackles into life and initially shows just the sofa and the wall opposite the dresser. Something heavy and metal is dropped off-camera, followed by a muffled conversation. Then there's a scream and the sound of someone struggling, followed by a door banging open. A young, female voice shouts for help, then there's a thud, followed by a low groan.

"What did I tell you, you stupid bitch," a well-spoken voice demands off-camera. "I told you to shut up, didn't I? I told you everything would be okay if you just shut your fucking mouth and stopped talking. But you wouldn't listen, would you?"

There is another thud, followed by a cry and a whimper.

"That's better, my sweet," the voice says in a mock-calm voice. "Just keep quiet now, and it'll all be fine. Now, why don't you come over to the sofa and lie down for me?" There is the sound of a struggle. "Trying to get away won't make it any easier, you know," the voice continues. "Bring her over here."

A teenage girl, tied at the wrists and ankles, is dragged into the frame by a thin man in overalls. The girl has bruises on her face and is clearly in pain. "Please don't hurt me," she begs in a hoarse whisper.

"You don't need to worry about that," the voice says. "Soon, you won't care what I do to you."

A small man in a checked shirt and tweed jacket steps into the frame. He has his back to the camera, but is clearly carrying a syringe. The girl looks up at him and then sees the camera. "No," she screams, "please, no."

The tall, bearded man switches off the camera and silence descends on the room. Distraught and shaking, he looks around, his eyes darting from side to side. He stares at the equipment and then back at the camera. Once he has gathered himself, he places the video camera carefully back in position and points it towards the sofa. He then zips up the hold-all and puts it back behind the sofa.

Back in the hall, he runs his hand back and forth through his hair, frowning and whispering to himself. He turns and stares at the front door, and then back to the kitchen. He then runs his hand over his clothes, still drying over the back of the chair. He frowns and looks up. Tucked in the top left corner of the hallway, half-hidden by peeling plasterwork and cobwebs, is another video camera. He spins around, and there is another, just above the main entrance. He rushes over to check them both, before putting them carefully back in their hiding places.

V

In the semi-darkness of the early morning, CCTV cameras, steady and impassive, watch the walkways, stairwells and bins of a tower block in south London. All is empty, silent and brightly lit. No one is to be seen.

The sun rises slowly over the endless rows of terraced houses, illuminating the patch of dusty grass and parking spaces in front of the block.

A middle-aged man, just out of bed, steps onto his balcony and smokes a cigarette.

A woman, still in last night's clothes, strides along a walkway, lifting her scarf closer around her neck to shield herself from the wind as she turns a corner.

A young man in a postal uniform climbs into a waiting mini-van, which drives quickly away as soon as the door closes.

A gull, drifting on the currents, glides across the face of the block, scanning for food.

As the sun begins to bathe the block in thin, autumnal light, Lauren, dressed in a pink Miffi vest top and loose combat trousers, emerges from a flat on one of the upper levels. She quietly, deliberately, closes the door, then glances left and right before heading for the stairs. She then runs down the open stairwell, trying to be as as quiet as possible as she pulls herself around each corner and launches herself down the next flight of stairs. Halfway down, Lauren stops to catch her breath, listening to see if she has been followed.

Drilling starts on a nearby estate.

A dog barks.

Satisfied she is alone, she continues down the stairs, slower this time and more careful to minimise the squeaks from her trainers. At the bottom, she places her hand on the door handle and waits. Nervous and breathless from lack of exercise, she breathes deeply to calm herself down.

Her hand is still on the door handle when it swings away from her. She jumps back in surprise. An old woman pushing a shopping trolley appears in the doorway. "Oh, sorry dear," she says, searching the young girl's face. "Oh, it's you, Lauren. How are you, my dear? I haven't seen you in an age. How's your mother?"

Lauren stares at the old woman and, saying nothing, pushes past her and walks quickly out of the door. "Give your mum my best for me," the woman calls after her as the door slowly closes.

Lauren walks briskly across the concrete carpark in front of the block towards an alleyway that runs down the side of the building. The man on the balcony flicks his cigarette away and returns to his flat.

IN THE ALLEYWAY, a man dressed in a checked shirt and tweed jacket stands next to a beaten-up old transit van. He impatiently checks his phone and looks up and down the alleyway. A woman with two children in tow pushes a pram past the end of the alleyway. She doesn't look up, but he turns away instinctively.

A bus roars past on the road.

Eventually, Lauren turns the corner and walks quickly towards the van, glancing behind her as she goes. As soon as he sees her, the man straightens up, his face darkening as she approaches.

"George," Lauren asks nervously.

"You're late," he snaps back, looking her up and down. "I thought you weren't coming."

"Well, I'm here now, aren't I?" She stares back at George, who shifts slightly on his feet. "You're older than I thought you'd be," she says. "And smaller."

"Really? And you're fatter than I thought you'd be. Are you getting in or not," he asks, nodding towards the van.

Lauren frowns. "How do I know you're who you say you are?"

"What do you mean?"

"I don't know who you are. Not really."

"Yes you do. We've messaged each other lots of times. You know who I am."

"But you could've been lying."

"About what?"

"Everything."

"Why would I do that?"

Lauren looks away. George turns to the van. "Just get in. We haven't got time to mess about. They're waiting for us."

Lauren hangs back, nervous. "But you could be anybody. Like a rapist or something."

George turns back, anger flashing in his eyes. "What?"

"How do I know who you are? You might want to rape me, or kill me."

"Don't be ridiculous. Why would I want to do that?"

"I don't know, do I? I don't know anyone like that."

They stare at each other.

"Okay, I'm sorry," George says eventually. Fumbling in his pocket, he produces a business card. "Here."

She reads it and turns it over. It says:

GEORGE CRANSOME
Producer
Locket Films

"Look, you don't have to do this if you don't want to," George says more calmly. "You can just say 'no' and walk away. That's okay. But then you wouldn't get to meet your father, would you?" He stares hard at Lauren. She swallows nervously and looks down. "Everything is set up," he says. "It's all ready. This is your big chance to finally meet him. Maybe your only chance. Ever." George steps backwards towards the van. "He would be so disappointed if you didn't show up, you know. He told me himself how much he's looking forward to meeting you. And you'd be letting everyone else down, people who've put in so much effort for all this to happen."

Lauren frowns. "Is...Is he really going to be there? For sure?"

"Of course he is. It's all set up, like I told you. He's itching to meet you, as a matter of fact. And the crew is on their way now. I just got a text from them." George lifts up his phone. "They might even get there before us."

"Okay," Lauren says quietly. "I'll come."

George gets into the van and Lauren walks around the front and gets in the passenger seat. She sits up straight and looks out of the window, but then slumps in the corner and looks away.

"Seatbelt."

She says nothing, but pulls the belt over her body and

clicks it into place. George stares at the girl, taking her in, while he starts the engine. The van then inches down the alleyway, bumping over the potholes and splashing in the puddles, and turns onto the main street. The van slowly makes its way across London, picking through the traffic as they head towards the A1. The sun is tepid, and the steam stays in the corner of the windscreen, despite the heater being on full blast.

George looks across at Lauren from time to time, who is still staring out of the passenger window. "Do you want to listen to some music?"

"No."

"It might make the time go more quickly."

"I said no."

George frowns. "I thought you'd be happier than this."

"What am I supposed to be happy about?"

"About all of this, about meeting your father," George says, exasperated. "You said you wanted to do it."

"Did I?"

"You said you were really looking forward to it. You said you've wanted to meet your father all your life."

"Yeah, well, that was then," she said, still staring out of the window.

"What's changed?"

"What do you think?"

"I don't know, Lauren. I really don't."

"Do I really have to say it out loud?" Lauren turns and stares at George angrily. "For fuck's sake."

"What?"

"I'm scared, aren't I? Really fucking scared." Lauren turns back to the passenger window, pushing herself further into the corner.

"Oh, right, I see," George says. "Right. Of course. Sorry." He flexes his fingers on the steering wheel. "Are you sure you don't want to listen to some music? It might help you to relax."

Lauren says nothing and they lapse into silence, ignoring each other as they pass the endless rivers of cars, vans and lorries criss-crossing north London, and then out onto the A1 proper and into the countryside.

"Sheep," Lauren exclaims happily and then falls immediately back into sullen silence. George glances at her, but says nothing.

THE VAN CARRIES on rolling up the A1, passing town after town, and overtaken by most of the other traffic on the road. Inside, the van is silent, save for the roaring of the engine.

George clears his throat. "I really did think you'd be more excited about this. I do appreciate that you're scared. It's only natural. But, still…"

Lauren stares at George. "You don't get it, do you?"

George shifts in his seat. "Apparently not."

A car towing a caravan overtakes the van, and Lauren and George watch in silence as it passes.

"I do hope you start getting excited, or at least happy about this soon," George says, glancing at Lauren. "Scared doesn't look good on camera. And you want to look your best for the cameras, don't you?"

Lauren fiddles with her fingernails, picking at the old pink varnish that covers most of her nails.

"You know, when we were messaging…" George says.

"Yeah, I know, I know, I know," Lauren cuts in impatiently. "I was excited then. Yeah, definitely. But now it's happening…right now. And all that about being on camera as well. I didn't think about it properly. I mean, my clothes…" She pulls at her Miffi top, which has ridden up over her belly. "And now, after all this time, I'm actually meeting him." She turns to George. "You know I've thrown up twice today? Twice. I tried to do it quiet so it wouldn't wake mum, but that just made it come out of my nose. It was totally disgusting." She looks out of the window.

"You didn't wake your mum did you?"

"No. I just said so, didn't I?"

"Good. This needs to be a surprise."

"I know. You said," Lauren says, exasperated. "I honestly don't know why I can't tell her, though."

"We talked about this already, Lauren. I told you it wouldn't work if you told her. And, anyway, your father insisted that your mum shouldn't find out, not until after you two met. It was the only way he would do this." George glances at Lauren. "He really wants to see you, you know."

Lauren turns away and looks out of the passenger window. "I've been thinking about what it'd be like to meet him all my life," she says quietly. "Every night, when I'm lying in bed."

"And now you are," George says emphatically.

"On TV," Lauren says. "You know my mum doesn't even have a picture of him? I don't know at all what he looks like. I mean, is he tall? Fat? Thin? Bald? I don't have a clue. I just know bits and pieces my mum told me from what she can remember." She turns back to George. "What does he look like?"

"Actually, I don't know," he says. "I haven't met him either. I've only spoken to him on the phone, so it'll be a surprise for both of us." George glances at Lauren, who looks disappointed. "He has a nice voice, though."

Lauren looks out of the window and laughs sardonically. "One shag with a guy she met in a pub. One shag in the pub toilets. You know she'd never met him before?"

"You said."

"No wonder she doesn't remember him. And she never

saw him again after that, you know. I don't even know if she remembers him at all. She just knows his name, that's all. Sam." Lauren sighs. "I mean. I don't know…She could have shagged the whole fucking pub for all I know. She says she only did it that one time, but she would say that, wouldn't she? Aunt Saffi says mum was a right slapper in her day."

"What about your mum's friends. What do they say about him?"

"They don't tell me anything. They just say it was a long time ago and I shouldn't bother about it. I mean, they don't know who dad was either, apart from him being some guy in the pub. Most of them weren't there that night, so they don't know him anyway. Mum's mate Bess says he was handsome and tall, but I suppose she could be just saying that to make me feel better." Lauren inspects her fingernails. "One shag in a pub toilet. And I come out. Like a big dump."

"Don't say that, Lauren. I'm sure your mother cares for you very much. I'm sure she loves you really, deep down."

"Yeah, well, maybe. But I bet she didn't love me at the time. She was only sixteen. That could be me in three years. Who would want that? It's a wonder she kept me at all. I'd have definitely had an abortion or put me up for adoption if it was me."

"Maybe your mum always wanted to keep you."

"You reckon? So you don't think she kept me because gran and grandpa are Catholic and they made her? Course she didn't want me. I was a fucking drag, every step of the way. She told me. She said I'd stopped her doing what she wanted to do in life."

"That's not true."

"Yes it is."

"But she doesn't mean that, surely?"

"So why did she tell me, to my face? She told me she never really wanted me and that I ruined her life."

Lauren stares at George. He glances across at her. "I'm sorry, Lauren. I'm sorry she told you that. It must've hurt a lot." Lauren sits back and glowers out of the window. "I'm sure she didn't mean it, you know. We all say things we don't mean when we're angry or frustrated."

"She wasn't angry," Lauren says quietly. "She wasn't even pissed, for once. Stone cold sober. She was just standing talking to me in the kitchen. Like you and me are now." Lauren sighs. "We'd just come back from shopping, and she hadn't been able to pay for it all. Again. She said that she'd have been fine if she hadn't been a mother, spending all her money on looking after me. That she could've had a life."

"She just stared at me, and she didn't know what to do. I was so upset and angry, I was shaking. For a second, I wanted to kill her. I wanted to grab a knife and stick it right through her. I wanted to rip her insides out. I was raging. But I didn't say anything. I just stood there, not knowing what to say." Tears roll down Lauren's cheeks. "She told me everything that's gone wrong in her life is my fault. Everything."

"Lauren, that can't be true, even if she sometimes thinks it is. And I doubt she really believes it. She's made decisions in her life and done things, of her own choice. She knows she has."

"Like what?"

"Like having sex with a man in a pub toilet," George says, shrugging. "That wasn't your decision. You didn't even exist then."

"Maybe. What difference does it make, anyway? The fact is, she doesn't like me and I'm a drag, holding her back, and there's nothing I can do about it. Nothing at all, except fuck off and leave her to live her life without me."

"You know, you're going to have to cut out the swearing when you're on camera."

Lauren laughs and poses. "Don't worry, I'll be all la-di-fucking-da."

They lapse into silence. After a while, George shifts in his seat. "So, do you think you might look like your dad?"

"I dunno. I don't look much like my mum, so maybe. I must've got my dark hair from somewhere." Lauren frowns. "Mum ain't a natural blonde, mind, but her hair is pretty light. You know, when it washes out and you can see her roots. And she's got this massive nose. I ain't got that." Lauren squints down at her nose. "My nose is quite small and nice, don't you think?"

George glances over. "Yes."

"And I've got these freckles. My mum ain't got those. Not on her face, anyway."

George shifts in his seat. Lauren looks out of the window and falls silent.

As THE VAN crosses another county border, Lauren turns to George. "Why did you look for me?"

"Pardon," George asks, concentrating on the road.

"Why did you look for me? How did it happen? Did he come to you first?"

"What do you mean?"

"How does it work? I mean, you can't have just found my dad randomly on the street and then come looking for me on the internet. He couldn't have even known he had a daughter?"

"Um, well…" George stammers. "Actually, he did know."

"What? How?" Lauren stares at George.

"Apparently your mum told him," George says casually.

"What," Lauren shouts, shocked. "What do you mean 'mum told him'?"

"I think she told him just after you were born. That's what

he told us, anyway." George pauses while Lauren stares, aghast. "He contacted us because he saw one of our ads. One of the ones in a local paper in Lincolnshire. He spoke to one of our researchers." George pauses, thinking. "Yes, that's right. He told us during that first interview. Your mum had definitely told him about you."

"What the fuck?" Lauren shouts. "What the FUCK?"

"She had…"

"When did she speak to him," Lauren demands, adding in a whisper: "She, she…"

"I'm not sure, to be honest. Definitely after you were born."

"She, she…" Lauren stares out of the window. "She lied to me."

"I'm sorry."

"She told me she didn't…that she'd never…she…That lying, fucking bitch," Lauren says to herself.

"Maybe you don't know everything about your mum's relationship with your dad after all."

VI

THEY CONTINUE IN STONY SILENCE. CLOUDS GATHER, AND THE
sky falls grey. Eventually, the silence is broken by the click-
click of the indicators, and the van pulls into a service
station. George drives twice around the car park before
settling on a secluded spot shaded by a knot of trees.

As soon as the van comes to a halt, Lauren flings her door
open and storms across the tarmac towards the squat, grey
building promising, in garish letters, fast-food, newspapers
and toilets. George watches her and then gets out of the van,
making sure all the doors are locked before following her.
Initially, he matches her brisk pace but, as she enters the
building, he checks himself and slows down.

Inside, George glances around, trying to spot her. There
are only a few people milling around between the newsagent,
the snack shop and the burger joint but he cannot spot her.
He walks into the newsagent and finds her looking at the
sweets and snacks. Unseen, he walks up behind her and
follows her as she searches the racks.

She stops and turns, almost walking into George. "What
the fuck do you want," Lauren demands in a loud voice.

George steps back, confused.

"Just back off, will you?" she says and turns away.

"Sorry," George stammers. She carries on around the aisles and George follows her again.

She stops and turns. "Look, leave me alone," she says, putting her hands on her hips. "I mean, what do you want? Really? What do you actually want," she asks, her voice louder with each question. A man and a woman by the till stare at them.

"I just don't want you to do anything rash," George says quietly, glancing at the other customers out of the corner of his eye.

"Rash? What does that mean? Like 'run away' rash?" George swallows. "You aren't my fucking mum, you know. Just leave me alone. Why don't you read a magazine? Something about cars or tits."

"Right," George says, trying to laugh it off. He glances at the other customers, who turn away and finish paying. He looks back at the racks of sweets. "I'm just trying to make sure you pick something healthy."

"What? Why do you care?"

"I want you to be healthy. In good shape…"

"For what? What are you talking about?" She looks George up and down. "You're so much less cool in real life." She pushes past George and goes to the till. As she turns her back on him, George's smile falls away and anger flashes across his face.

After paying, Lauren heads to the toilets, George following at a distance. She stops at the entrance and faces him. "Are you going to follow me in here as well?"

George pulls a pained expression. "No. I'll wait here."

"Suit yourself."

Lauren disappears into the ladies. George notices a tall,

well-built family man glaring at him. George smiles weakly. "Kids, eh?" The man turns away.

VII

They drive the rest of the way up the A1 in silence. Deep grey clouds obscure the sky and the air hangs heavy with the coming rain. The evening rush hour has begun, and the roads fill with commuters heading home.

The van slows and a huge articulated lorry roars past them.

They peel off at the next exit and drift away from the main roads and into the autumnal decay of the countryside. They drive further and further away from towns and villages, past endless fields interspersed with hedgerows and knots of trees.

Partway down a narrow road between fields, the van slows and turns onto a dirt track. Slowly, gingerly, the van eases off the road and onto the track, weaving and bobbing along its uneven surface towards a small copse with a run-down cottage partially hidden within. A flock of birds, picking through the freshly ploughed soil, rises into the air as one as the van approaches.

The van enters the copse. Tipping and pitching across the uneven ground, it slows to a halt right in front of the cottage.

George pushes open his door, which lets out a tired creak. He drops out of the van and onto the muddy ground, and looks around in satisfaction, his hands on his hips.

A crow caws in the distance.

He surreptitiously pulls a remote control out of his pocket and presses a button before slipping it back out of sight. He then turns back to the van and motions to Lauren to get out. She stares at him with a look of disgust on her face. After a few seconds, she opens her door and hesitantly steps onto the muddy earth. She adjusts the straps on her Miffi vest top and resumes staring at George.

"Where is this place? It's freezing."

"I told you to bring a coat," George says, glancing around.

"Whatever."

"Well, in any case, this is it. We're here."

Lauren looks around her. "You're kidding me. This dump? Here? We're in the middle of nowhere."

"Maybe, but it's still the place."

"I don't believe you."

"Why not? Your father chose here. He wanted to meet you here. I presume we'll find out why when he gets here."

"Bullshit."

"No it isn't." George squares up to her. "You do still want to go through this, don't you? We haven't come all this way for nothing, have we?"

Lauren steps back. "If this is the place, then where is everyone?"

George says nothing but pulls out his phone. "Ah yes, here we go. They're on their way. They must've texted while we were driving. The film crew, and your father, they're all on their way. Judging by when they sent this, they shouldn't be no more than half an hour or so." George smiles and puts his phone back in his pocket.

Lauren glances around again. "I…This just can't be the

right place," she says quietly. "I mean…I didn't imagine…" She pulls her arms tight around her body. "It's freezing."

"I told you it'd be colder this far out of London."

"Yes, but I just can't believe that this place…that he would have…"

"Suit yourself," George says as he turns away. "It's still the right…" He stops and frowns, then stares up at the attic window above the main door.

He waits.

A pigeon flies out of a hole in the roof above the window. George relaxes and smiles. Lauren narrows her eyes as she watches him. Glancing back at Lauren, George says cheerfully: "As I said, it's definitely the right place. It's where he said he wanted to meet. He was very particular about it, as a matter of fact." Motioning to Lauren to follow him, he adds: "Come on, let's go inside. We might be able to make a fire or something while we wait, and then we'll be toasty warm."

Lauren watches him walk away and sticks out her tongue. "As if we could be warm in this dump," she says to herself, before reluctantly following him inside.

THE FRONT DOOR of the cottage swings open and George strides in, with Lauren trudging a few paces behind. George walks around the hall, checking the doors. He stops in the middle of the hall and looks around, puzzled. He draws his foot across the boards and frowns. He notices the fire has been used. He bends down and places his hands over the ashes. After a few seconds, he stands up. He is at eye level with a picture on the mantelpiece. George frowns and picks it up, examining it front and back.

"What the hell is this place," Lauren asks, her voice shaking. "It's, like, totally abandoned. It's like no one lives here. What's going on?"

Brought back to his senses, George turns and stares at her intently. "What do you mean?"

"This house…It isn't right. I've got a bad feeling about this. We shouldn't be here. Why did you bring me here?"

"Lauren…"

"No. No more bullshit, George. No more of your bullshit. This isn't right, and I want to leave. Right now."

"Look, Lauren," George says, stepping around to block her way to the front door.

"No," she shouts. "I want to leave. Take me back to London. I want to see my mum."

George slams the door shut. "No, Lauren. It's too late for that."

"What…What do you mean," she asks, her voice shaking. "Let me go. I want to go home." Lauren runs for the front door but George catches her. He wrestles with her and then throws her back into the room. Lauren, shocked into silence, stumbles back into the middle of the room and gathers her composure.

"Look, Lauren," George says breathlessly. "I an assure you that you have absolutely nothing to worry about. Please believe me."

"But this place…" she says, looking around. "It ain't right. I don't like it."

"You have to believe me."

"Why? Why should I?"

"You have to trust me, Lauren."

"No, I don't want to. I won't."

"Look, Lauren, I don't want to spoil the surprise but there are very specific and important reasons why your dad chose this place to meet." Lauren frowns. George runs his hands through his hair. "This place…it apparently has some significance to him that will become clear when he gets here."

"But…I don't understand."

"I know, Lauren. I know you don't understand. Me neither. But it's all okay. I promise you. Just wait. Just wait and see when your father gets here. You'll see. Everything will be fine."

Lauren leans on the back of an armchair by the fireplace and looks around again. George sighs and goes back to the picture on the mantelpiece. He is about to examine it again when he hears a door opening behind him. He spins around to see Lauren entering the room by the main door.

"Don't go in there," he bellows.

Lauren stops and turns around slowly. She still has her hand on handle.

"What? What the fuck is wrong with you?"

"I said don't go in there."

"Why not?"

"It's not safe for you in there." Lauren stares at him suspiciously. "The crew told me not to let you go in that room. It's not safe. It's something to do with the ceiling." George takes a deep breath. "Look, I'm sorry I shouted, Lauren. It's just that it's not safe for you to go anywhere else in the house other than in here or the kitchen. I just want to make sure you're alright, okay?"

Lauren closes the door and wanders back into the middle of the hall. She spots one of the video cameras on a shelf and stares at it. "What's this?"

George glances over his shoulder. "What? Oh, that. It's for the film crew."

"That's not a proper film camera. My uncle's got one of these. If he's got one, it must be shit. What's it for?"

"What? Oh, it's just for testing out the shots. You know, to help with placing the real cameras when the crew gets here. And they're not rubbish, actually. They're very high quality, with excellent sound recording." George stares at Lauren, who looks unconvinced. "We sometimes use them for filming to get a different type of shot. Like of someone arriving somewhere. Into a building or room. You know, a bit like a CCTV picture, but much better quality, and then we can add the visual effects to it later."

"And you left it here? It could've been nicked." Lauren looks at the camera more closely. "Hey, it's switched on."

"Is it?" George says offhandedly. "Someone must've forgotten to turn it off."

Lauren reaches out to grab the camera.

"Don't touch that," George shouts angrily.

"What? Why not?"

"It's important," he says more calmly. "Okay? It's for the crew."

"I just wanted to see…"

"Well don't. Leave it alone." George points to the middle of the room. "Just stand there, will you? Stand still and try not to touch anything."

Lauren shuffles away from the camera and mumbles to herself. "What's got into you? You're worse than my mother. Ordering me about. Not letting me into rooms, not letting me touch the stupid camera, not…"

"Look, Lauren, this has to go properly, okay? Everything has to be just right from the beginning, and you doing things wrong will only screw it all up."

"What do you mean? There's no one here but us. What does it matter what we do now? We haven't started yet."

"It just has to be right, that's all. You'll see." Lauren frowns and kicks at the floor. "Look, just stand there and don't touch anything. Okay?" George stares at Lauren, then walks over to the room next to the main door and opens it.

"Hey, how come you can go in there when it wasn't safe for me?"

"I'm in charge, that's why," George says before disappearing into the room.

"Twat," Lauren says under her breath.

Inside the room, George immediately looks down the back of the sofa. He checks that the hold-all is still there and rummages around inside to make sure everything is in order. He straightens himself up and smiles. He then checks the camera on the dresser opposite and makes sure that it is working. Satisfied, he goes over to the window and looks through a gap in the curtains. The copse is still and silent, and the road can hardly be seen.

He turns back and strides quickly out of the room, slamming the door behind him. Lauren is still standing in the middle of the hall, holding her arms to her chest against the cold. George smiles at her but she doesn't react. "We should get a fire going," he says, cheerily. "You're never going to get warm if we just stand around like this."

On the back stairs, George and Lauren's muffled voices can be heard faintly. The tall, bearded man is on the landing, listening intently.

He starts to pad gently down the stairs but forgets about the loose step, making it squeak loudly as he steps on it. He freezes, cursing himself, and waits.

Their muffled voices carry on as before. After a few seconds, the man continues down the stairs.

"So when are they getting here?"

George pauses on the threshold of the kitchen. "Um…" He pulls out his phone. "Ah, yes. Here we go. I just got a text from them, actually. They say they'll be here in ten minutes. They've asked us to put the kettle on. I don't think there's any electricity here, but we'll do our best. What do you want? Builder's tea?"

He smiles at Lauren but she just shrugs and stares back. "You know, you should start to enjoy this, Lauren," he says. "This is your big moment."

"Whatever."

George shakes his head and laughs. As he turns back towards the kitchen, a shadow flashes behind him and something swings towards his head.

"Look out," Lauren shouts.

George frowns but, before he can turn, he is struck heavily on the back of his head. He lands awkwardly, blood already seeping onto the floor. Lauren stares at him, shaking with fear. The tall, bearded man steps out from the shadows, a large wooden table leg in his hand. He tilts his head, staring at Lauren from under his brow.

"Don't hurt me," she whispers.

THE WHITE ROOM

I

THERE IS ONLY THE BILLOWING WHITE EMPTINESS OF A BRIGHT and crisp morning. A distant calmness, constantly flowing through endlessly shifting shades of perfect white. An impenetrable bright, white mist; soft and enveloping. All is tranquil; all is clean and pure.

The shifting rush of a waterfall, or the rustling of sheets. A woman, half-awake, half-asleep, stirring in this half-world of luminescent perfection. Her skin, soft and pale, melts into the white, enveloping light.

She is there and not there, slowly sensing herself as the billowing emptiness coalesces around her.

"Were you asleep," a male voice asks from somewhere beyond.

She feels her feet as they slide underneath the clean, pure, white sheets.

"No," she says softly. Her arm glides and she places her hand on her soft, pale skin. "Yes," she corrects herself, "I was. Did I talk?"

"No, not this time. But you were…agitated. I was a little worried."

"Thank you." She smiles to herself, relishing the sound of his words floating through the misty, enveloping whiteness.

Her fingers catch on the sheet and she slowly pulls it down, over her head and below her chin. The room is bright white, lost in the mist, just the hint of a picture frame somewhere in the distance.

She becomes aware of her body, twisted and thrown open across the bed. She straightens herself and slides her head back on the pillow.

"Are you awake," he asks, his voice drifting away from her.

"Mmmm." Her voice is echoless in the mist, faint, floating from nowhere.

"Did you dream?"

"No. Nothing."

EVERYTHING FADES TO BLACK.

In the darkness, light rain falls on a cobbled street. Footsteps run. A car drives slowly past. Café music strikes up. An accordion. Laughter and the tinkle of glasses.

A light breeze, and she moves, skipping lightly across the road towards the music. As she approaches, the music slows down, slower and slower, until it grinds to a sickening halt.

Now there is nothing, just emptiness.

"No," a woman's voice calls out. "No, no."

"Are you okay?" The man's voice, gentle, concerned, drifts across the blackness from somewhere beyond.

She falls silent.

THE BRIGHT, white and enveloping light returns and her body moves once again under the sheets.

The room, filled with mist, more treacherous now, returns to her.

"Was I asleep?" Her eyes open a little.

"Yes, you were. I think you were having a nightmare."

She closes her eyes. "What time is it?"

"Seven."

"Do you want to hear about my dream?"

"Don't I always?"

She stares at an empty picture frame on the wall. The room is white, almost without end. Hard, bright white.

"I dreamt a lot, I think. I can't remember most of it."

"Do you remember anything?"

"Mmm…"

"Try and think. Anything at all."

She shifts under the sheets and looks away. "There is one dream I can remember quite clearly. I've had it before, a long time ago. I think I might have already told you about it."

"Go on."

The rustle of sheets as she moves, trying to find a place of comfort, to recall the feeling of the enveloping bright, white mist.

She sighs. "It was a dream about dreaming. In it, I can feel myself, just before I wake up. I'm bathed in sweat and exhausted, lying asleep in my dreamworld. But just before I wake from this dream within a dream, I can see myself lying in a peaceful room. Not this one, but a room in an old house, a bit like the one I grew up in. It's full of old furniture. There are knick-knacks lying all around and photos in frames on the walls. It's full of things from someone's life, but not mine."

She pulls the sheet closer to her.

"There's a soft light coming in from behind muslin curtains. And I'm lying there in the bed. Asleep. I'm so still, so calm. You know, I can even see a smile on my face."

The man frowns and pushes his glasses back up his nose. He thinks for a moment and then makes some notes on a piece of paper.

"I can see that I'm asleep in this dream, but my eyes are open. And I look into my eyes, right inside, deep enough to see my dreams. There, I can see scene after scene of happy, beautiful people walking along cobbled streets that are dancing with light after the rain. It looks like Paris, near Le Marais, the way it was all those years ago when I first started going there. And I'm happy. I'm happy lying there asleep in my bed, dreaming. It's the happiest time of my life."

She stares at the ceiling and frowns.

"But then darkness starts to seep in from the corners of the room, like a black cloud pushing its way into this perfect moment. Slowly at first, and then quicker and quicker, the darkness fills everything, choking out the light. I reach out to hold on to this calm, perfect, happy me, but I'm torn away and I start screaming."

A tear rolls down her cheek.

"I can feel myself choking, as if the darkness has reached around me and is squeezing my throat and filling my mouth. I know I'll never see that perfect, happy me again. It's so painful. It's as if the dream is a child being ripped from my arms."

She sobs quietly, staring at the ceiling.

She turns to the man. "What do you think it means?"

II

The woman shifts on the bed and its white-painted metal frame creaks against itself. The room is lit by blue-white neon and the grey-white of a winter sky flooding in through the metal-framed window.

Outside, a van beeps as it reverses.

She looks up at the thin white cord hanging from the ceiling and remembers the last time she pulled it. She shudders away from the memory, from the panic, the fear, the powerlessness. And the pain that she nursed for weeks afterwards.

She gazes across at the man sitting on the fold-out chair by her bed. His hair is crisp and precisely combed, and his rectangular glasses seem severe to her. His white coat is neat in its ironed perfection. He flicks through his notes, all on headed notepaper and countersigned.

"What do you think," she asks.

He shifts in his chair. "Well, in some ways, it's obvious." She waits, expectantly. "But of course there are so many ways of interpreting these things," he says finally.

He turns over a page and then quickly flicks through

several sheets before putting down his clipboard and smiling at her.

"But it doesn't really matter what I think. What do you think it means?"

She sighs and turns away, staring at the endless grey-white clouds billowing across the sky.

III

"Hello? Hello, yes, it's me."

"No, I've seen her today, just now in fact."

"Yes, she's fine, I think. Making progress."

"No, not yet."

"I think you're going to have to be patient. She is very fragile at the moment. I don't want to push her too far too quickly."

"No, of course. I realise that. I know you'd rather we got results fast..."

"But I don't want to break her completely. I don't want her to become permanently ill. I just want her to think that she's ill, not for her to become irretrievable. Anything else would be unprof..."

"Yes, I know that none of this is professional, but to do that to her would be..."

"No, no. She doesn't seem to remember that at all."

"To be honest, it's hard to know what she actually thinks, deep down inside..."

"Yes, I know I'm a psychiatrist, but even we don't have a window on..."

"I'm sorry, but I can only go on what she tells me."

"No, I don't think that's necessary. I think they're working well at this dose. She is already unstable and seems pretty afraid of the outside world. I think if we let nature take it's course, then…"

"Of course. I'm aware that you want the documents signed and it all finished, but it's not just me who can do that for you. I can get her to that point, but an independent second opinion is needed to satisfy the requirement that she's no longer capable…"

"Yes, but that means her condition needs to be real and consistent, and she has to recognise herself that she's a…"

"I'm sorry, could you repeat th…"

"What do you mean?"

"But this week is too soon."

"Oh, I see. Well, if you insist…"

IV

The woman lies in the bed, staring at a shadow on the opposite wall, trying to imagine it as a picture frame. The folding chair is gone.

The room is suffused with a soft, hazy brightness, and she is drifting in and out of the enveloping mist. She is a boat moored in an endless, white ocean, drifting back and forth with the tide's rolling swell.

She pulls back the sheet in one fluid movement and reveals her naked body. The coolness of the air brings her out in goosebumps and she shivers. She runs a hand over her soft, pale skin, feeling the bones pushing through.

She places a foot on the floor. The tiles are cold, and she lets the chill creep up her body. Eventually, she pulls herself upright and steps out of bed. She steadies herself and then walks over to the bathroom in the corner of the room.

She sits on the toilet, perching her feet on the balls to minimise the cold. A memory drifts across her mind and her face crumples.

She forces herself to urinate, pushing the liquid out from her, listening to the splashes echo around the tiny, cold room.

She turns on the shower and waits for it to heat up before stepping inside.

She cleans herself, slowly, deliberately. The suds slide across her skin and the steam rises up around her. She drifts into the clean and white mist, falling through the billowing light. She pushes her hands down her thighs and flicks her hair, arching her back and squeezing her muscles tight. She runs her hands between her legs and pulls a finger heavily across her clitoris.

But she feels nothing and her face remains calm and impassive.

The walls of the shower become rough against her skin. The water lurches perpetually from hot to cold, and the cheap shower gel irritates her. Coldness seeps in from the room, tugging at her, pulling her back.

She turns off the shower and grabs a thin, rough towel. She dries herself slowly, deliberately. As she passes the bathroom mirror, she sees a flash of make-up and a sparkling cocktail dress. Who was that?

She stops and goes back into the bathroom, but all she sees in the mirror is her gaunt, pale body. Her thin breasts hang down over her ribcage.

V

THE ROOM IS A WHITE, SPARSE BOX, FILLED WITH STARK, NEON light. The clouds outside the window are heavy and grey, sucking out any warmth.

The door to her room opens and she pulls the towel tight around her body. The man walks in, carrying her notes, looking at the floor. When he looks up, he is surprised to see her standing in front of him.

"Oh, so you're up. You fell asleep again before I left. Did you dream this time?"

"No, nothing," she says, shifting uncomfortably on the cold tiles.

He smiles. "Never mind. Maybe next time." He examines her face and frowns. "Are you all right? You look a little disturbed."

She swallows. "Am I still the same person, the one who came here all that time ago?"

The man gazes back her blankly, waiting.

She glances at the bathroom and then back at him. "I caught myself in the mirror just now and I didn't recognise myself. I'm so thin." She looks down at her body poking through the towel.

He nods. "You are thinner, there's no doubt about that. But you're still the same person." He shifts slightly on his feet. "You know, you were very unhappy when you came to us, but you seem so much calmer now."

He motions for her to sit down and she perches on the edge of the bed, the sheet still half-thrown over the side and trailing on the floor. He brings in a folding chair and sits down. He sighs and opens her notes. On the front page is her name, date of birth, date of admission and current status. He flicks through a few pages, arriving at a medication sheet.

He looks up. "I've been thinking. You seem a little agitated at the moment…I think we might want to increase the dose of one of your drugs."

She smooths the bedsheet by her bare leg. "If you think it's necessary, doctor."

He stares at her, inspecting her face. She avoids his gaze.

"Do you think you might be ready to leave, to go out there again?" He gestures towards the window. "You do know that you can leave at any time you want? Whenever you're ready."

She glances at the window and then back at him with fear in her eyes.

"No, I don't want to leave. Not yet."

DEATHCAST

It had been thought, until our time, that tyranny was a hateful thing in whatever shape or form. But at the present time we have discovered that there are legitimate tyrannies and holy injustices as long as they are exercised in the people's name.

— ALEXIS DE TOCQUEVILLE, 1835

PATRICK SSKB578 GLANCED AROUND THE RUN-DOWN PUB. The windows were covered with metal grates, and the only illumination came from the occasional battered lamp. There were few other customers and they gathered in small knots in the darkest corners of the room, talking together in hushed tones.

"Are you sure they won't pick us up?" Patrick looked up at the barman, who was cleaning a glass with a towel, and nodded towards the door.

"No, I'm sure of it. In here, we're basically in a Faraday cage. Plus we put some false signals outside the building so it doesn't look like there's an anomaly when they do a sweep of the street."

"But what about this?" Patrick jerked his thumb towards his neck.

The barman shook his head and put down the glass. "Nothing I can do about that. You geocasted before you got here, right?"

"Yes, of course."

"So it should just work as normal then, just with the location data pulled from something else. What did you use this time?"

"Jack's dog."

The barman laughed. "I'm sure he's enjoying having an excuse to take the dog out for a walk. So, what can I get you?"

"I dunno. What have you got?"

The barman pointed at a rusty old fridge standing in the corner. "We've got some of that stuff you had last time, when we were in that other place, and then something brewed up by Mick. You remember him? The guy from the West Country. He says he knows how they did it the old way."

"Oh yeah, I remember him." Patrick nodded to the row of taps in the middle of the bar. "So you haven't managed to get those working yet, then?"

The barman shook his head wearily. "Nope. Not yet. I don't know what's wrong with them, to be honest. Mind you, it would help if I knew how they worked in the first place."

"There must be a book about that lying around somewhere."

"True. But where? That's always the question, eh? Anyway, what'll it be?"

"I think I'll try some of Mick's stuff."

"Right you are." The barman pulled a bottle out of the fridge and flicked off the metal. "Glass?"

"Nah, it's okay."

Patrick took a swig of the beer and savoured its taste before swallowing. "That's all right. Almost tastes like the real thing. Mind you, it would help if I knew what the 'real thing' was actually like."

"Yes, it's not bad, for what it is. He says he used the original recipe, or as close as he could get, and he bottled it himself."

"How did he manage that without anyone getting suspicious?"

Before the barman could answer, the door of the pub was kicked open and several armed police in heavy body armour and face masks stormed into the pub.

In a panic, the customers, including Patrick, tried to get away, knocking over tables and chairs in the search for another exit, but they were soon cornered. At gunpoint, the police forced them to the ground and restrained and hooded them, before dragging them away.

Unseen, the barman slipped away into the dark recesses of the pub and disappeared.

CHAPTER TWO

PATRICK HALF-WALKED, HALF-STUMBLED INTO A BRIGHTLY LIT laboratory, led by two men in white coats. He was extremely unsteady on his feet and could barely lift his head, which was pounding with a brutal headache.

As he lurched from side to side behind the two men, he caught glimpses of the rest of the room. On one side appeared to be a large, raised viewing platform behind reinforced glass, in front of which were several rows of large chairs arranged in a semi-circle. The rest of the room was more like a laboratory, packed with computers, sensors and equipment, with other people in white coats milling around.

Several drones drifted and turned around a large camera dome in the ceiling, while two heavily armed guards in body armour and face masks patrolled the edge of the room.

Patrick was led to a chair at the edge of the semi-circle, and fell heavily into it. He watched helplessly as the two men placed his feet into foot rests and strapped his ankles to the chair, before doing the same with his arms.

The two men walked behind the chair and Patrick tried to struggle as they placed a brace over the top of his head and a strap around his chin and neck, pulling it tight. Finally, they placed a thick strap around his chest, making all but the smallest movements impossible.

The two men walked around to the front of the chair. Patrick struggled violently and stared wildly at the two men. He tried to shout, but his mouth was held shut, and all he could do was groan.

The older of the two men folded his arms and tilted his head to one side, a smile playing on his lips. "Don't worry, Patrick. You are Patrick SSKB578, yes?" A flicker of recognition pass across Patrick's fearful eyes. "Good. I am doctor MDPY332, or John, if you prefer, and this is my assistant," he said, waving a hand at the man standing next to him.

John looked at Patrick, who was still struggling, and frowned. "I feel sorry for you, Patrick. It turns out that your friend at the pub was not really your friend after all. I know you tried your best to throw us off the scent. It was very clever of you to transfer your geolocation data, but it turns out that good old-fashioned intelligence is sometimes more useful than all that modern technology." The doctor let out a small laugh. "So much effort, Patrick, put into keeping yourself hidden in plain sight. I wonder why you do it." He stared at Patrick and sighed. "Still, it is not my place to care too much about that. I am here merely to make sure that you are kept as comfortable as possible until your turn comes."

John turned to his assistant, who had been waiting patiently by his side. "Perhaps we should begin." The younger man began to prepare a large syringe on the trolley by Patrick's chair. Patrick stared at the needle in panic. Noticing his expression, John said cheerily, "Don't worry, everything will be fine. It's not like the old days, you know. Back then, we used to do all this without sedatives." John frowned. "It was barbaric, all things considered. Do you know, one person died of shock, right in front of me, and we lost several even before we reached the coup de grâce, so to speak. Mind you, it's not so surprising, if you think about it."

Noticing his assistant was nearly ready, John said, "But don't you worry, this won't hurt one bit. In fact, you won't feel a thing. You'll just feel nice and relaxed. Cosy, almost."

The assistant turned around with the large syringe, now full of dark, glistening liquid. "Thank you," John said as he took it.

As the needle approached, Patrick struggled and strained against the straps holding him down. The assistant held one of Patrick's arms steady and the doctor slowly injected the entire contents of the syringe.

After a few seconds, Patrick stopped struggling. The fear fell away from his eyes and a look of placid emptiness spread across his face.

"Could you put in the retractors, please," the doctor asked.

The assistant pulled open Patrick's eyes without any resistance and placed in metal eye retractors, followed by several drops of anaesthetic.

"Thank you."

John checked Patrick's eyes and measured their diameters. He went over to the equipment area of the laboratory, and returned with a device similar to a pair of spectacles but with the lenses replaced by thick metal discs attached to heavy cables. The insides of the discs were covered with millions of fibre-optic cables, surrounded by a circle of tiny hooks.

The doctor checked the size of the discs against Patrick's eye sockets before pressing them in firmly until he felt the give of the hooks piercing the cornea beneath and hooking into his eyeballs. Patrick tried to move his head but could only murmur in protest.

Satisfied that the discs were fixed in place, the doctor went over to a control panel and switched it on.

EVERYTHING IS BLACK.

A few scattered lights flash in the darkness.

A swirl of patterns in rich, evocative colours emerges from the nothingness and then spreads slowly outwards, shimmering and evolving as it grows, filling everything.

The swirls settle down into a slightly off-kilter and distorted procession of disconnected stylised memories—fields; sunsets; children playing together in a back garden; a young boy running up a street; blowing out candles on a birthday cake; countryside passing on a long car journey—all in an endless loop of comforting images.

In the background, the Andante from Mozart's Piano Concerto No. 21 strikes up, bringing a perfect glow to the perfect memories, fading and jolting with the distortions, as if it's being played back on a warped tape.

The visuals roll on and on and on, one after another, in an endless, peaceful sequence of idealised recollection.

CHAPTER THREE

Poppy was asleep. All around her, in her small, box bedroom, was a jumble of toys, posters, clothes and games.

She woke instantly, unsure why, and stared at the camera dome in the middle of the ceiling.

The door opened and Maggie, dressed in a thin, grey bathrobe, walked in. "Good morning, darling. How long have you been awake?"

Poppy said nothing but carried on staring at the camera dome. Maggie glanced at it and then back at her child. "It's time you got up, young lady. It'll soon be time for school."

"Okay mum," the young girl said emptily.

Maggie closed the door and Poppy listened to her footsteps as they receded along the corridor and down the stairs. When she could no longer hear her, Poppy waited a brief moment longer and then got out of bed.

Straightening her pyjamas, she walked into the brightly lit bathroom adjoining her room. On the wall opposite the door was a sink with a large mirror above it and, in the middle of the ceiling, a small camera dome.

As Poppy stepped into the bathroom, the mirror flickered

into life and messages flashed up wishing her a good morning and informing her that she had thirty minutes until the school bus arrived. It also reminded her that she had two sets of homework to hand in that day.

Poppy barely noticed the screen, which switched from showing messages to data on her current height and weight, as well as her blood pressure, heart rate, blood cholesterol levels, and levels of markers of systemic inflammation. It also presented her current estimated risk of several diseases, and showed how she was performing against a series of targets for daily and weekly diet and exercise.

Poppy cleaned her teeth and inspected her face in the parts of the mirror not covered with text. She thought about going to the toilet but looked up at the camera dome and decided she wanted to wait until she got to school.

Maggie, dressed in a simple, unflattering uniform, was wiping down the kitchen worktops when Poppy walked in. The room was plainly furnished, with a counter and a couple of stools. In the centre of the ceiling was a camera dome, and the entirety of one wall was a touch screen. It showed the current time and weather, with a five-day forecast, alongside the ten last incoming and outgoing calls and texts and the family to-do list. There was also a news ticker running across the bottom of the screen listing the latest government achievements and announcements. In one corner of the screen was a map, with a home icon in the middle. There was also a pop-up showing a photo of Poppy and another of Maggie, each with a pin showing their current location as being at home.

As Poppy pulled herself onto one of the stools, the screen changed to show several messages addressed to her:

School Bus A15 arriving in 15 minutes
Prepare school bag for today's lessons. See Timetable for more
details

<u>Updates to Timetable</u>:
Assembly to sign Pledge of Perpetual Allegiance and Wellness
Contract brought forward from tomorrow to today, at 0815
Wellness and Social Responsibility discussion to follow
All other morning lessons suspended.
Afternoon timetable unaffected.

Poppy read the messages, watched surreptitiously by Maggie. She then sighed and turned away from the screen.

"What's the matter, my darling," Maggie asked. "Didn't you sleep okay?"

"No. I had nightmares." Poppy leaned on the counter, resting her face on her hands.

"Oh dear. I am sorry, sweetheart. That's not very nice." Poppy said nothing and stared straight ahead. "Why don't you have some breakfast now," her mother asked. "It'll make you feel better."

Maggie turned on the kettle and opened a cupboard with row upon row of identical plain boxes, each stamped with 'Nutrimix' and a Wellness Department logo. Selecting a box, she pulled out one of several identical, plain sachets containing a thick, grey powder. The kettle clicked off and Maggie tipped the powder into a bowl and stirred in the hot water until it reconstituted into a paste. She then passed the bowl to Poppy and placed a spoon beside it.

Without reacting, Poppy started eating and Maggie went back to cleaning the kitchen. As Maggie was scrubbing the sink, she noticed a drone floating outside the window. Instinctively, she turned away.

"Where's dad," Poppy asked, between mouthfuls.

Maggie glanced up at the camera dome in the ceiling.

"Have they told you anything, mum?"

"Ssh," her mother hissed. "Don't talk about that."

"But I want to see him," Poppy said loudly.

Maggie went up close to Poppy. "I'm sorry, my love," she said quietly in her ear, "but we can't talk about that here." Maggie glanced up at the camera dome and Poppy followed her gaze. "I know you're upset, sweetheart, but talking about it won't bring him back, and it'll only make things worse for us."

The young girl looked down and fiddled with her spoon.

"Please, Poppy. Promise me you won't breathe a word about any of this at school? We don't need any more attention." Poppy stared into her mother's eyes. "Do you promise me?"

The girl nodded slowly. "Okay, I promise."

"That's my girl," Maggie said, trying to sound bright and happy. "You finish your breakfast up now and you'll be set for the day." Maggie noticed an alert flash up on the touch-screen. "Oh, look, your bus will be here in a minute," she said, trying to hold her voice steady. "Hurry up and eat your breakfast, or you'll miss it."

Poppy quickly finished the bowl and dropped her spoon inside.

The screen announced:

School Bus A15 arriving in 25 seconds. Poppy to go to Bus Stop C

"Come on, my darling. Get your bag. It's time to go to school."

Poppy dropped off the stool and walked into the hallway. Her mother followed her and grabbed her coat, helping her into it as they walked to the front door together.

As Maggie opened the door, Poppy picked up her

schoolbag and turned back to her mother. They looked at each other in silence, neither sure what to say, before Poppy ran down the path to the gate and out into the street.

Maggie closed the door behind her and sighed heavily. She glanced up at the camera dome in the middle of the ceiling, and then walked back into the kitchen.

The touchscreen announced:

Poppy boarded School Bus A15 at 0748

The Poppy icon on the map showed her moving away from home, along the main road. Another message flashed up:

Maggie:
Agitated mood and mild tachycardia detected
Blood pressure increasing and stress hormones released
Take Position A, 2 metres from screen

Maggie dragged a stool in front of the wall screen and sat down. The kitchen lights dimmed and the touchscreen changed into a large, swirling, shimmering, pulsating pattern of colour and light, accompanied by a comforting hum.

After a few seconds, Maggie began to settle down and her breathing became regular. She slipped slowly into a trance.

CHAPTER FOUR

THE SCHOOL BUS PULLED UP OUTSIDE A NONDESCRIPT SET OF gates, which opened onto a concrete yard in front of a long, squat building. Heavily armed guards in face masks patrolled outside and inside the gates, while several drones drifted back and forth over the yard. There were no teachers present, although camera domes lined the top of the building.

The bus doors opened and two dozen young girls, including Poppy, ran down the steps and into the schoolyard, where they dashed around and played noisily with several dozen other girls who had arrived on earlier buses.

The school gates closed behind them.

A disjointed, metallic voice rang out, "All children will line up in front of Entrance B." Without hesitation, the girls stopped playing and lined up two-by-two in front of one of the doors into the building.

"All children will now enter the school," the voice said. The door swung open with a hiss and the girls, now completely silent and expressionless, filed in to the building. Once they had all entered, the door swung shut behind them.

Inside the building, the children filed past an empty reception desk and along a corridor leading to the school hall. As they entered the corridor, a metal frame running along the floor, up the walls and across the ceiling switched on. A blue light ran continuously along its length, flashing each time a girl passed.

Armed guards milled around in the corridor, glancing at the pupils as they processed towards the hall.

In the hall, each girl found her designated seat in the rows set aside for her class. They calmly and quietly took their place. As each girl sat down, a light flashed in the back of the seat and a small screen displayed their name and a green tick.

Heavily armed and masked guards milled around in the aisles by the side of the hall and two drones circled around a large camera dome in the ceiling above their heads. The stage was empty, aside from a small lectern with a microphone to one side.

After a few seconds of complete silence, broken only by the creaking boots of the armed guards pacing up and down, a stern middle-aged woman in a simple, unflattering uniform walked out of a side door and onto the stage.

The girls applauded politely and in complete unison, clapping exactly forty-five times each as the woman took her place, before lapsing into complete silence.

The woman looked out at the children, taking them in. "Good morning, children," she said in a clear, flat voice into the microphone.

"Good morning, Head Teacher," they called back in perfect unison.

She waited a few seconds. "As you will be aware from the morning alerts that you received this morning, there has been a change to today's timetable."

"Yes, Head Teacher," the children called back.

"Your timetable has been altered so that you can benefit

immediately from two important facets of your life to come. I am talking, of course, about your Pledge of Perpetual Allegiance and your Wellness Contract."

The woman paused and looked around the room, ensuring that she had the full attention of every girl present.

"You will all be well aware from your recent lessons that complete Wellness is not only the ideal state for us as individuals but also your main duty in life. After all, there can be no pleasure without responsibility. Moreover, all pleasures that we enjoy must, and I emphasise 'must', promote the Wellness both of the individual and of our society as a whole."

She reflected. "One could say that, as reward and pleasure both take from the vessel of life, one must make sure that that vessel is filled at all times. Filled with virtue, with good health, with wellbeing and with duties fulfilled."

"Yes, Head Teacher," the girls chorused back.

"As you get older," the woman continued, "there will be times when you find that achieving the right balance between your personal life and your responsibilities, both to yourself and to society, is more or less difficult. There will also be times when you find it more or less difficult to prioritise your Wellness and responsibilities over the desire for personal pleasure."

"No, Head Teacher," the girls exclaimed in unison.

"Yes, children, I'm afraid so. Hard though it may be to believe now, one does not always find it so easy to choose the correct and virtuous path in life."

She paused to glance around the room.

"It is for that reason that, today, you have the wonderful opportunity to sign your personal Pledge of Perpetual Allegiance. This, as you know, is an allegiance to yourselves, to the people, to the nation and, of course, to our glorious leaders, whose only objective is to help you to maximise your contribution to society.

"In addition, you will, today, be fitted with your personal gift: a Wellness Chip. This will, alongside the Care Chip that you had fitted at birth, be your lifelong guide and guardian in the pursuit of Wellness, helping you to ensure you stay always on the right path, the virtuous path, and make the right choices to place your Wellness above every other consideration."

"Thank you, Head Teacher."

The woman smiled. "Now, children, I think we are ready, so if you could line up in front of the stage..."

The girls, including Poppy, left their seats and quietly formed a neat line, while the Head Teacher motioned to the side of the hall. A guard opened a side door and a man and a women dressed in plain uniforms walked to the front of the queue of children.

For each child in turn, one of the officials ran a scanner up the back of the child's neck. As the scanner beeped, the name and full details of the child appeared on a tablet. The tablet then presented a personalised version of the Pledge of Perpetual Allegiance, followed by the Wellness Contract, which each child signed on the tablet screen. Once the signatures had been registered, the other official held a gun-like device to one of the children's wrists, which, with a jolt, inserted a smooth, white plastic capsule under the skin and then sealed the wound.

The children winced, but said nothing.

The official then placed the device over their ribcage, next to the heart, and another capsule, this one in bright blue, was inserted under the skin and, again, the wound sealed. As before, the children tried not to react, despite the obvious pain. The scanner was then run over both insertion points, each beep registering on the tablet, with the serial number of the devices confirmed as having been assigned to the child.

Once the officials had finished, each child waited in line on the other side of the stage, all watched with quiet satisfaction by the Head Teacher.

As Poppy approached the front of the queue, a girl in front of her hesitated before signing the Pledge.

"What's wrong," the official holding the tablet asked.

The girl looked up at her nervously. "I don't want to sign it."

"Why not," the official asked calmly.

"My parents don't want me to."

The official cocked her head to one side and frowned. "Why would that be, young lady?"

"They say it's wrong to sign it at our age. They say we should wait until we've grown up and then decide whether we want to sign it or not."

"I see." The official looked up at a nearby guard, who approached and then waited quietly to one side. "That's very interesting…Bea," she said, checking her tablet. "Look, Bea, I am happy to discuss this with you and talk about your parents' concerns, but we have a lot young ladies to get through this morning. So would you go with my friend, here," she asked, motioning towards the guard, "and we can talk about this as soon as we've finished everyone else. Okay?"

The girl looked up at the guard, who towered over her in his body armour and mask, and started shaking. "There's nothing to worry about, Bea," the official said kindly. "I'll only be a minute and then we can chat." The guard jerked his gun towards the door and Bea walked slowly away from the line. As he opened the door to let the young girl through, she looked sadly back at her school friends, and then walked through, the door closing silently behind her.

"Who's next," the official said, and Poppy stepped forward.

The other official ran the scanner up the back of Poppy's neck, which beeped as it passed.

"Hello…Poppy," the first official said. "How are you?"

"Fine, thank you."

"Good." The Pledge of Perpetual Allegiance flashed up on the screen, which Poppy signed, followed by her Wellness Contract.

"Thank you, Poppy. And now for your Wellness Chip. Which arm would you like it in?"

Poppy looked confused. "I don't know."

"Do you eat with your left or your right hand," the official asked.

Poppy looked down at her hands. "Um, right."

"Let's go for the left, then."

The other official held out Poppy's left hand, and Poppy glanced up, fear in her eyes. "Don't worry. It releases a special chemical as it goes in that means you won't feel a thing," he said. "You'll feel nice and relaxed. Cosy, almost."

Poppy swallowed and the official pulled the trigger, firing the white capsule into her arm. He then placed the device over her chest and the blue capsule was shot under her skin. Tears welled up in Poppy's eyes, but she said nothing. The scanner was run over the insertion points, which beeped and the devices registered.

"There we go. All done," the first official said.

She smiled at Poppy but the young girl simply walked away and joined the back of the other line.

Eventually, every child had signed the contracts and had their chips inserted. They then filed out of the hall and down an empty, undecorated corridor, with guards posted at either end and several drones drifting idly around the ceiling. They passed windowless classrooms full of younger children sitting in perfect rows, perfectly still. Some called out chants to the teacher at the front, while others were sat in semi-darkness, lost in a trance, staring at huge, shimmering, glowing images swirling and coalescing on a giant screen. In each classroom, at least one drone turned perpetually around the camera dome in the middle of the ceiling.

Poppy and her classmates turned a corner and passed a classroom of older girls. They were sat calmly and diligently working on tablet screens, while a teacher walked up and down between the desks, checking on their work as she passed. Finally, they reached their own, unadorned class-room and they quietly, unhurriedly found their desks.

The teacher, dressed in a similar uniform to the girls, was sitting at the front of the class, reading on her tablet. Behind her, a giant touch screen covered almost all of the wall. As each child took their place, their name flashed up on the screen as being present, as well as on a tablet screen embedded in the top of their desk. Once the last child had carefully closed the classroom door and taken her place, the screen showed that all pupils currently scheduled to be at the class were present and the class could begin. Bea was listed as absent.

The room was silent, aside from the soft hum of the drone floating overhead.

The teacher looked up. The girls were all sitting quietly at their desks, looking towards the front of the class, patiently waiting for the lesson to start. Satisfied, she stood up and waked towards the middle of the room. She gestured towards the touch screen, which changed to show a series of bright and colourful images of happy people exercising in sunny parks, running along canals, playing beach volleyball, enjoying walks together. Across the images, the screen read:

The Pursuit of Wellness

"As you are aware, today is a special day for you all," the teacher said. "It is your first day of being full members of our society." She paused and turned back towards the front of the room. "But with that honour comes responsibility, and chief among the responsibilities that you have taken on today is that of prioritising and safeguarding your health and wellbeing, for the benefit of both yourself and wider society. In other words, the pursuit of Wellness."

"Yes, miss," the girls chanted in unison.

"With that in mind, I would therefore like you all to repeat the chants that we learned last week."

The teacher touched the wall screen and a rolling text appeared, mirrored on the tablet screens embedded in the children's desks, with a dot above the word to be chanted. "Now, children, after me." The teacher turned to the class and raised her arms as they called out a series of chants extolling the virtues of Wellness. Poppy stumbled over the words, and had to check her tablet repeatedly.

Once they had finished, the teacher sat on the edge of her desk. "Well done, everyone. Now, can anyone tell me some of the things you can do yourself to promote your Wellness, which, as we all know, is the greatest gift that we can give ourselves?"

A young girl shot her hand up.

"Yes, Jenny," the teacher said.

"Regular exercise," she asked.

"Yes, very good, Jenny. Anything else?"

Several hands shot up. The teacher pointed at a girl sat towards the back of the class. "Yes?"

"A balanced diet?"

"Yes, Elisa, excellent. A balanced diet. But what, exactly, does that mean, a 'balanced diet'?" The teacher got up and started pacing around the room. "As you know, every family in our nation is provided by our benevolent government free of charge, a perpetual supply of Nutrimix, which all of you will have had this morning for breakfast before coming to school."

"This, if your parents haven't explained to you already, is a powder that, when reconstituted, provides all the nutrients, proteins, carbohydrates, fats, sugars and amino acids that you could ever need, as well as the daily recommended dose of fibre. It was created many years ago as a replacement for old-fashioned foods like meat and vegetables, which were problematic because their nutritional value was unpredictable. With Nutrimix, we know exactly what the body is receiving with every single mouthful, and we know that, by eating it, we are all maximising our health and wellbeing. So, children, there is absolutely no excuse for anyone in our great nation to be anything other than perfectly nourished, with a balanced and nutritious diet. All thanks to your glorious leaders."

The teacher stopped and looked around the room. "Now, can anyone tell me anything that would harm Wellness; something that could put your special and treasured health and wellbeing at risk?"

There was no response from the girls.

"Come now, ladies, you must know some activities that have been banned by the Department of Wellness as being contrary to the achievement of our personal Wellness targets."

A girl put up her hand slowly.

"Yes, over there," the teacher said.

"Smoking tobacco?"

The teacher broke out in a smile and nodded her head. "Yes, indeed. Thank you. Smoking tobacco. But you must remember that it's not just tobacco we're talking about. Smoking anything at all puts your Wellness and that of those around you at risk. It is an evil habit that leads only to illness and death."

The teacher glanced around. "Anything else?"

Jenny raised her hand tentatively.

"Yes. Jenny."

"Alcohol, miss?"

"Thank you. Yes, alcohol," the teacher said. "Now, Alcohol, ladies, comes in many, many forms, but no matter what form it takes, it is nothing more than a poison. It poisons the mind, it poisons the body and it poisons the soul. And it turns upright citizens into nothing more than craven dissolutes who think only of meaningless pleasure."

"Oh, no," the girls chorused in unison.

"Yes, ladies, we must guard always against its consumption, wherever you see it. And the same goes for tobacco. Wherever you see either of those evil poisons, you must report it to the authorities immediately. Whether it's your parents, the parents of your friends, or just someone you see in the street or in a social situation, you must always make sure that it gets reported, so that we can all be protected against these dangerous substances, and such people can be protected from themselves."

The teacher let her words sink in.

"Anything else?"

Another pupil raised her hand, and the teacher nodded for her to speak. "Fatty foods?"

"Yes, young lady. Fatty foods are a menace, and that is why they were banned without exception." The teacher glanced around. "What about you, Poppy? You've been unusually quiet today. Do you know of anything else that could damage your Wellness?"

"Um," Poppy said, looking down at her tablet.

"Come on, Poppy, it's not difficult."

Poppy thought for a moment and then, relieved, said, "Sugar?"

"Yes, thank you, Poppy. Indeed, sugar. As I am sure you all learned in your history lessons, sugar, particularly white, refined sugar, was identified several centuries ago as being linked to illnesses such as diabetes, obesity, heart disease and certain cancers. Not only that, but it is a highly addictive stimulant that corrupts the body and the mind. Of course, we struggled for a long time to get it banned, as there were so many commercial interests intent on making addicts of our children at a young age, and it took years of effort to finally pass the necessary legislation to have it banned. Did you know, ladies, that, in some parts of our glorious nation, merely the possession of one ounce of refined sugar can mean arrest, or worse?"

The children looked at each other, impressed by the weight of the teacher's words.

"When you think about it, the whole question of Wellness is very simple. Anything that promotes your Wellness is to be valued, while anything that puts your Wellness under threat is a crime both against yourself and against society, pure and simple. The reason is that the very fabric of our society rests on you, each and every one of you, pursuing your Wellness above and beyond all else."

The teacher stopped and turned to face the room.

"You need to learn all of this by heart, girls. It is part of your Contract with our society, and is the ideal by which we all live. Of course, that makes anyone who isn't promoting that ideal a threat to us all."

She continued, "So, anyone who is caught doing things or helping someone else to do things that can harm their Wellness will, without exception, be Corrected."

The girls looked at each other, shocked to hear the word said out loud.

"And for repeat offenders? Does anyone know what will happen to them?"

The teacher looked around the classroom, waiting for someone to raise their hand, but there was no response.

"Poppy?" The teacher stared straight at her, and she involuntarily sat up. "Do you know, Poppy, what happens to repeat offenders?"

"No, miss."

"Well, I shall tell you, young lady. Repeat offenders will be Corrected. Permanently."

CHAPTER FIVE

IN THE KITCHEN OF THEIR MODEST HOME, MAGGIE CLEANED away breakfast. The touch screen showed the Poppy's location as being at school.

As Maggie was wiping down the kitchen counter, the screen showed an alert:

Elaine HWC391 approaching the front door

The doorbell rang and the screen showed a CCTV image of a woman beside the front door, next to her name. Maggie looked up at the screen and frowned. She put away her cleaning cloth and wiped her hands on the sides of her trousers as she went to the front door.

Elaine, who was dressed in an almost identical outfit as Maggie but with a handbag hanging from the crook of her arm, stared blankly at Maggie as she opened the front door.

"Why don't you come in," Maggie said, turning away and walking back to the kitchen.

Elaine carefully closed the door behind her and followed

Maggie down the hall. "How are you, Maggie," Elaine asked, as she perched on a stool by the counter.

Maggie leaned on the sink and stared at Elaine, trying to read her expression. She glanced up at the camera dome.

Elaine said, "I mean it, Maggie. How are you, really?"

"I'm fine thanks," Maggie said in a cheery but brittle voice. "And you?"

"Are you sure you're okay? Have you heard anything about Pat…"

"I'm fine," Maggie said, cutting across Elaine before she could finish the word.

"Well, if you're definitely okay," Elaine produced a small paper bag from her handbag and placed it on the counter in front of her, "then you won't want one of these."

"What have you got there," Maggie asked. She leaned forward and placed her elbows on the counter.

Elaine neatly rolled down the sides of the bag, a smug smile on her lips. "Only some chocolates I managed to get hold of, that's all."

Maggie recoiled and stepped back. "What the hell are you doing," she demanded in a hoarse whisper.

"What do you mean," Elaine asked innocently.

"You know exactly what I mean. Bringing those things here…Aren't I in enough trouble as it is, without this?" Maggie jabbed her finger up at the camera dome. "You do know they're watching our every move and listening to every word we say, don't you? I mean, you haven't gone completely mad, have you?"

"Maggie, love, they're not going to be bothered about something as trivial as a few lumps of chocolate every now and again. Anyway, I've met my Wellness quotas for this week. I deserve a little reward."

Elaine waggled her fingers in anticipation and then

picked a small ball of chocolate, dropping it into her mouth and luxuriating in the melting pleasures.

Maggie stared at her, open mouthed. "Elaine," Maggie insisted.

"What," Elaine asked, her mouth still full.

"Do you really think they don't care about 'a few lumps of chocolate'?"

"Of course not."

"And what about the Wellness Contract? What's that all about, then? Just a few bits of paper?" Elaine shrugged. "And what about all this?" Maggie gestured around the room. "All this stuff they provide for us?"

"What of it?"

"Think about it, just for a minute," Maggie said, tapping the side of her head. "It's jobs, money, housing, food, every-thing. They give us everything…I can tell you, Elaine, they do care about what we say and do, and about what we eat. They care about it a lot, because they give us all this, and they don't want see all that investment they make in us going to waste. And if they do catch you, us, with that stuff lying around, we'll be in serious trouble."

Elaine swallowed the rest of the chocolate and placed her hands on the counter. "Okay, yes, maybe you're right. Maybe they do care what we get up to and what we eat."

"Exactly."

"But only within reason." Maggie frowned. "What I mean is: They care, but they aren't stupid. They only go after big people who do really bad things. They don't waste their time going after small fry who bend the rules a little bit from time to time."

Noticing Maggie's doubtful expression, Elaine continued, "Look, it's a waste of time and resources to go after people like us. We're not worth the effort. If they do decide, however, that you're a threat then, of course, you're in serious trouble. Otherwise, they leave you alone, and you can do pretty much anything you want."

Maggie shook her head in disbelief.

"This lot don't waste their time and energy on people like us," Elaine said. She sighed and glanced down at the chocolates. "You have tried chocolate before, haven't you?"

"Yes, of course I have," Maggie said, indignantly. "Just not in a while, that's all. Where did you get them from anyway," she added, stepping back over to the counter to take a closer look.

"Sources."

"Sources?" Maggie said, smiling. She glanced up at the camera dome. "Anyway, you shouldn't take them out here, right underneath one of those. You'll definitely get us into trouble doing that."

"For a tiny bag of chocolates like this?"

"It's like you're flaunting them," Maggie said. "After all, you know what it says in the Contract: No substances or foods that could place your Wellness at risk."

Elaine laughed. "At risk? What's so wrong with a bit of chocolate every now and then? Anyway, doesn't it lower your heart risk?"

"That's cocoa and, anyway, we get all of that sort of stuff in the Nutrimix." Maggie looked exasperated. "Come on, you and I have both been told this stuff a thousand times before…chocolate contains refined sugars and fats, and they cause diabetes and heart disease. It makes you unfit, unproductive. Plus, chocolate releases endorphins."

"What's wrong with endorphins? Exercise releases endorphins."

"But chocolate is a 'fake stimulus'," Maggie said impatiently. "It's an unnatural high. And you know it's bad for us to have excessive agitation. They've told us that."

Elaine looked at Maggie incredulously. "What? You actually believe all that stuff?"

"Look, Elaine, it doesn't matter whether I believe it or not. It's what they tell us, and that's good enough for me." Maggie looked into Elaine's eyes. "Do you want them to take you away?"

"Don't be ridiculous. They aren't going to do that."

"Don't be so sure. I've heard of people being taken away just for talking like we're doing now, let alone actually eating a banned substance."

"Please don't worry," Elaine said, placing her hand over Maggie's. "It's fine. I talk like this, and more, at home all the time and nothing, nothing has ever happened to me. No warnings, no phone calls, nothing. Like I say, they won't take you away, Mags, if you're not a threat to them."

Maggie stared at Elaine and then her face crumpled, a tear rolling down her cheek. "Was Patrick a threat, then," she asked quietly.

"I'm sorry, Mags, I didn't mean..." Elaine got up and put her arm around Maggie's shoulder.

"I know. It's just...Patrick and I, we never do anything we shouldn't, we never say anything we shouldn't, and we certainly never buy anything we shouldn't," Maggie nodded towards the chocolates, "not even something like that. And yet they still..." Maggie started to sob.

"Have you heard nothing at all," Elaine asked gently.

Maggie stood up and walked over to the sink, drying her eyes. "No, nothing." She looked up and noticed another drone hovering outside the window. She turned away and leaned on the sink.

"He just didn't come home one day. No-one knows anything. No-one at the factory, no-one at the bus company that brings him home...I even asked that thing." Maggie gestured to the touch screen, which was saying that Elaine had been present for ten mins and twenty-three seconds and that Maggie's blood pressure was high. "But it never replied, even though I know the question was uploaded. It's almost like he never existed, you know? I thought they were supposed to tell you if they did something to your family?"

Elaine shrugged her shoulders. She pushed the bag of chocolates towards Maggie. "Are you sure you don't want one of these?"

Maggie sighed and walked over. She placed her elbows on the counter and her chin in her hands, staring down at the little sweets. "So you really don't think they'll take us away if we eat one?"

"Nah. I don't think they'll even register it. Anyway, I've already had one, and they haven't said anything to me."

"What about the breath analyser."

"Not interested."

"What? It isn't interested or you aren't interested?"

"Both," Elaine said, smiling. She tugged at the side of the bag. "Do you want one of these or not?"

Maggie sighs. "I'd better not."

"Suit yourself. Just means more for me."

Elaine picked the biggest chocolate in the bag and popped it in her mouth, a grin spreading over her face as it melted.

"All right, all right," Maggie said. "I'll have one. But only one."

Maggie rummaged around in the small bag until she found a chocolate she wanted and popped it in her mouth. She smiled, in spite of her best wishes.

"How's the endorphins," Elaine asked.

They both looked at each other and laughed.

Once she'd eaten the last bit of her chocolate, Maggie stared at the bag, lost in thought. "The worst thing about all of this is what I'm supposed to tell Poppy. It's not like she hasn't noticed that her dad has gone missing. What can I tell her?"

Elaine was about to answer when an alarm went off and they both turned to look at the touch screen. The screen was flashing red, which faded and a message flashed up:

Poppy picked up from school in official car
Poppy arriving home in 5:00 minutes

The time immediately started counting down. Maggie and Elaine exchange worried glances.

Another message flashed up:

Poppy to be fed on return home
Maggie and Poppy will then board Transport Bus B78 at 1415, Bus Stop D

The wall screen returned to its usual mix of weather, recent calls and texts, and government news, except that the pin showing Poppy's location was moving steadily towards the Home icon. The time was 1342.

"What's happening," Maggie asked Elaine in a panicked voice.

"So far? Nothing," Elaine said, trying to sound calm.

"But she's been sent home from school. What has she done? And why do we have to take a bus?" Maggie burst into tears.

"Look, Mags, there isn't time for crying. It's probably nothing at all. Just some routine thing that you've forgotten about, that's all."

"Really," Maggie asked, looking into Elaine's eyes.

"Of course. I bet you it's nothing serious it all. Now, you start getting yourself ready and I'll get some Nutrimix ready for Poppy to eat when she gets back, okay?"

"Okay, thanks, Elaine," Maggie said, squeezing her friend's arm. "I really don't know what I'd do without you."

"Me neither. Now, get yourself ready."

Maggie disappeared to her bedroom, while Elaine grabbed two sachets of Nutrimix from the cupboard and put the kettle on to boil.

The wall screen announced:

Poppy arriving

The screen showed Poppy, in her school uniform, walking up the path to the front door. A drone hovered in the background of the picture.

"She's here," Elaine called out.

Maggie appeared from the bedroom with a fearful expression on her face.

"Now don't you start panicking, Mags. That won't help anyone and you'll only end up making her panic too. And then neither of you will be any use to anyone."

The doorbell rang.

"Mags, everything will be fine," Elaine said, "but making her scared won't help one bit."

"Okay." Maggie straightened her clothes and went to the front door to let Poppy in. "Hello darling," Maggie said, trying to sound as bright as possible. "You're back home early. Is everything okay?"

"Yes, mum," the girl said seriously as she stepped into the house and took off her coat.

"So why did they send you home?"

"I don't know."

"Are you sure you didn't do anything or say anything," Maggie asked nervously as she hung up her daughter's coat.

"No mum. They just called me out of Citizenship Class

and said I needed to take the bus home." Poppy looked up at Maggie. "What's happening? Is this to do with dad?"

Maggie stroked her daughter's hair. "I don't know, sweetheart. Why don't you go into the kitchen and eat your lunch. We've got a bus to catch soon."

Poppy walked into the kitchen. As soon as she saw Elaine, she ran over and gave her a hug. "Auntie Elaine," the girl exclaimed.

"Hello my poppet. How are you? Everything okay?"

"Yes, I think so."

"Good." Elaine glanced up at the screen. "Right, you've only got five minutes, so you eat your lunch while we get everything ready, okay?"

Elaine pushed the bowl of warm Nutrimix towards Poppy, who grabbed a spoon and started eating. Meanwhile, Maggie finished getting ready. She fumbled over her shoes and then tugged at her hair with a brush as she stared blankly at herself in the hall mirror.

Elaine walked over and stood beside her. "Try not to worry, Mags," she said quietly.

Maggie glanced over at Poppy, who was eating her Nutrimix quietly. "What's going to happen to us?"

"I don't know, Mags. No-one knows what's in the future. We don't know yet why Poppy was taken out of school today, or why you're going on that bus, so there's no point in trying to second guess any of that. Just be as positive as you can and everything will work out in the end."

Before Maggie could respond, the screen announced:

Transport Bus B78 arriving in 35 seconds
Maggie and Poppy to go to Bus Stop D

A panicked look flashed across Maggie's face.

"Don't worry about tidying up," Elaine said quickly. "I'll do all that. You two go and get your bus."

"Thank you, Elaine, I appreciate it, and everything you do for me."

"Shut up and go, or you'll miss the bus."

Maggie nodded. "Come on, Poppy, time to go." Poppy dropped off the stool and ran over to her mum. "Grab your coat and let's go, my lady."

"Okay." Poppy snatched her coat from the stand and they both ran out of the door and down the path, followed lazily by a drone. "Bye-bye, Auntie Elaine," Poppy called back over her shoulder.

"Bye-bye, my poppet," Elaine said to herself as she closed the front door.

She walked slowly back into the kitchen. The screen flashed up a message:

Maggie and Poppy boarded bus B78

Elaine cleared up the kitchen. As she was leaving, she stopped and glanced back at the family knick-knacks and mementos scattered around the sparsely decorated house. She sighed and then left, slowly pulling the door shut behind her.

CHAPTER SIX

IN THE INFINITE BLACKNESS, THE SWIRL OF RICH, EVOCATIVE *colours and idealised memories rolls on and on and on—children playing with a garden hose on a brilliant summer's afternoon, spraying water everywhere; the glistening of a pink and white ice cream eaten at the beach; the pitch and twist of a rollercoaster; the winning flourish in a game of Snap—on and on and on, glitching and warping now and then. Mozart fades in and out, but plays endlessly, the perfect soundtrack to the perfect memories.*

Sporadically at first and then more insistently, the stream of memories starts to glitch, and a series of other images cut in, chopping and pushing their way across the roll of memories in jagged lines.

Eventually, the music falls silent and the swirling colours fade, leaving only darkness.

From the shadows, Patrick walks along a dark and empty street in a run-down part of the city. He looks around as he walks, checking to make sure that he's not being followed.

There are no streetlights here, and the rats scurry noisily between the buildings, knowing they will not be disturbed.

He slows down at the entrance to an alleyway and checks his watch. Midnight. One more glance around and then he walks down the alleyway, disappearing into its moonless shade.

At a nondescript, semi-hidden doorway covered in graffiti, Patrick knocks and waits. A red light switches on and a camera lens appears. Patrick looks up and down the alleyway. The door unlocks and opens slightly. Patrick pushes it open and steps inside.

IN THE LABORATORY, Patrick, still strapped tight into the chair, was agitated and struggling. The cables leading from the metal discs inserted into his eyes were shaking.

The doctor came over to the chair. His assistant was already standing watch over Patrick, with a large tablet cradled in his hands. Multiple readouts and charts filled the screen. A drone hovered nearby.

"What's wrong with him," the doctor demanded.

"He's having a physical reaction to something," the assistant said, glancing down at the tablet.

"I can see that," the doctor said. "But 'why' is the relevant question."

The assistant glanced up at Patrick, who had sweat pouring down his brow, and back down at the tablet. The young man hesitated.

"Well? What is it," the doctor demanded. "What's the data showing? Is he having a heart attack?"

"No, no he isn't," the assistant said tentatively. "I don't know…It seems from the brain wave data that he might be having unregulated thought patterns."

"What do you mean? That he isn't mirroring our programming anymore?"

"It seems not, sir." The assistant checked something on the tablet. "It looks like he's broken free of the programme and is thinking for himself. He's having his own dreams."

The doctor frowned. "Hmm, interesting. Have you tried changing the program?"

"Yes, twice. We're already using the most complex one, as we knew he'd be a difficult subject."

"Okay. Have you tried increasing the doses?"

"Yes. We've done that as well. We've gone almost as high as we can." The assistant hesitated. "I didn't want to go any higher because I didn't want to risk Correcting him by mistake. Not before the visit this afternoon."

"No, of course not," the doctor said, thoughtfully. "Okay, we'll do this: Increase the dose of the brain peptides by 0.05 ml/kg per hour. It should just stop him being able to recollect his own memories, but not quite enough to Correct him."

The assistant looked doubtful. The doctor looked around to make sure no-one was listening and that the drone was not flying close by.

"Look, between you and me," the doctor said, "as long as he's even vaguely still here, it doesn't really matter what state he's in. They'll never notice the difference. And, anyway, we've mined all the data we'll ever get from him. We can't learn anything new now. He's basically just a shell. So just increase the dose and we'll leave it at that. Okay?"

"Yes, sir," the assistant said. "I'll get onto it right away."

The doctor gave a troubled smile and walked away, while the assistant tapped on his tablet and occasionally glanced up at Patrick.

Patrick pushes slowly through a curtain and enters a dimly lit room that clearly used to be a pub. A few people are gathered in small knots in the darkest corners.

The barman is inspecting the taps in the middle of the bar.

Patrick glances around the room, checking who else is there, before making his way over to the bar.

He runs his hand over the wood of the countertop. The varnish is coming off in places, and there are the tell-tale holes of a woodworm infestation.

"I heard you were serving tonight," Patrick says, glancing at the barman.

"So they say," the man replies noncommittally. "Are you here to meet anyone?"

"Maybe." Patrick pauses. "How long have you been here?"

"We opened last week. It took a while to get the word out. You know how it is."

Patrick nods, lost in thought. He glances around the room again, searching the faces of the other customers.

"Are you sure they won't pick us up here?" He looks up at the barman and nods towards the door.

"No, I'm sure of it. We're basically in a Faraday cage..."

Before the barman can finish, the pub starts to judder and shake. The image of a child running across a field of wheat lurches across the scene, and then disappears. In the far distance, the Andante from Mozart's Piano Concerto No. 21 strikes up.

"...inside..." the barman slurs as the pub warps and blisters.

From a swirl of rich, evocative colours, a child catches a ball and smiles into a golden sunset; a dog jumps and licks a young boy's face, its tail wagging in excitement; a rich and succulent peach is picked from a tree in a misty orchard.

In the background, Mozart plays on an endless loop, the perfect accompaniment to the perfect memories.

CHAPTER SEVEN

In a workshop full of computers, network cables, lathes, electric saws, welders and electrical equipment stacked in untidy piles, a group of people, all dressed in identical, plain overalls, lounged around a battered desk, lit by a bare bulb.

"So, what happened to him," a man with dark, curly hair and glasses asked.

"He got picked up two days ago, in a makeshift pub, of all places," a tall bond-haired man, who was repairing an old circuit board, replied. "Apparently, the police were doing a raid and he got caught up in it."

"So what do we know," the first asked.

"Well, we know they haven't killed him," the other replied. "Not yet, anyway," he added, raising an eyebrow.

"Where are they holding him," demanded a well-built man with a shaved head.

"Apparently he's in one of the Correction Labs in the Department," the blond-haired man said, adding in a sarcastic tone, "Waiting to be made an example of, I shouldn't wonder."

"What an idiot," chimed in a woman with short-cropped hair and an angular face. "Why on earth would he be so stupid as to risk going to a pub?"

"But isn't that exactly what we're fighting for here," the dark-haired man asked. "Aren't we fighting for the freedom to do what we want with our lives, including having a drink in a pub?"

"Maybe, but there was too much at stake for him to risk getting caught by the police like that."

"Actually, there's a lot at stake for all of us. And, you know what? If we wait until we've won the fight and we're all free to do those things, we may never get to do them."

"Whatever," the woman said. "The reality is that, however he got caught, it's all over for him now."

"Why," the blond man asked, surprised.

"What do you mean 'why'? His brain will be fried by all those drugs they inject them with, and his eyes ruined by the metal discs. By now, he's a zombie, as good as dead. What use is he to anyone, let alone us?"

"I'm not so sure," the blond-haired man said. "We've cleaned people up before, got them functioning and living a normal life, and we can even repair his corneas nowadays."

"So what," the well-built man asked.

The blond-haired man shook his head in disgust. "I can't believe you can say that."

"Look, we don't need another 'normal' man kicking around. We need someone who can help us, and help the cause. That's all that matters."

"So you'd just let him die, would you, and be forgotten? He's done a lot for us, you know. He deserves better than just being abandoned."

The well-built man turned to another women with shoulder-length red hair and green eyes. She was leaning back on her chair with her foot on the table, apparently not listening to the discussion. "What did he know about our current operations," the man asked.

She straightened up and shrugged. "I don't know. Not much, I think. We hadn't briefed him about the next stage. He knew a lot about what we've done already, of course. And about us." She looked around at the other faces staring back at her.

"It doesn't matter," the well-built man said.

"How can you be so sure," asked the blond man, putting down the circuit board.

"Look, it's very simple," the well-built man said, placing his hands on the table. "By now, they know whatever he knows. They'll have drained his brain and processed every thought, every memory, every idea he's ever had. Everything he has said and done will be on their computers and scoured for any piece of information that is useful to them. The fact that we've not been picked up already or killed means either they're planning to get us all at once in some big sweep, or that we all did our jobs properly and ensured that none of us knew enough about anyone else to be able to compromise the organisation. After all, we don't know anything about our lives and we don't even know each other's names, and, thankfully, they can't extract faces from memories yet. So to rescue him now would not only be a waste of time and effort but would place us all in danger, effectively for nothing, especially as he can no longer be of any help to us in his current state."

The room fell silent.

"I disagree," the red-haired woman said eventually.

"Why? On what basis?"

'I don't think he's necessarily irretrievable, and I think he could be useful to us in the future."

"Well, that's your opinion."

"In any case, I don't think we should just leave him there," she continued. "It's not right. We have the capability to get him out of there, and I think we should show the authorities that we can strike right at their heart."

She pointed around the room. "The time of us skulking around in the corners, hoping for a small victory now and then before we go running back into hiding, has to be over. We will never, ever overthrow the government and set ourselves free if we don't start doing something significant, something that will actually hurt them. So far, we've been like wasps, hoping for an occasional sting that might itch for a while but then is quickly forgotten. No, enough of that. We have to damage them, properly. We have to damage them so that they can feel it, and we have to show them we're a force to be reckoned with. And, if we're talking about rescuing him, I think that's the perfect place to start."

The well-built man stared at her in disbelief and shook his head. "Okay, Ms Superhero. Great. Brilliant idea. Of course, let's do it. Now. I mean, why not? What are we waiting for? Would could possibly go wrong?"

She stared at him in stony silence.

"Oh, yes, of course. I know what's stopping us," he continued. "He's a prisoner in a Correction Lab deep in the Department. Even if we could get in there without being detected, which is a very big 'if', how on earth would we get him out? They've got metal detectors everywhere, so we wouldn't be able to take any guns with us. What would we do to them? Drown them in Nutrimix?"

No-one laughed or even smiled.

"It's impossible," he said eventually, pushing himself back into his chair.

The dark-haired man with glasses took a deep breath. "Actually, I don't think it is so impossible."

The others turned and stared at him.

"Go on," the well-built man said. "Wow us."

"Okay. Well, you know how we all got here tonight, without being detected? We used geocasting, right?"

"Yeah, apparently I'm sitting at home watching TV with the dog," one of them said.

"Exactly. So, we all know how that works: we take the geolocation data of someone or something that has an unregistered Care Chip, typically in a dog, and we cast the geosignal from our own Care Chip into it with handheld beamer, so that when the drones are looking for us, because the unregistered chip is now associated with our chip's serial number, they assume that is where we are."

"Yes, that's all obvious so far," said the short-haired woman, "but how could that help us to get him out of a Correction Lab."

The man scratched his head and pulled a face. "Well, the thing is, we've been working on something," he said. "It's actually what I was about to tell our friend about before he got caught…"

"Well? What is it?"

"It's a bit of an 'upgrade' of the geocasting idea." He paused and frowned. "Okay, keeping it very simple…As you know, we can all be Permanently Corrected at any time via one of the drones, if they receive a termination order."

He glanced around the room to make sure everyone was following him. "Basically, if the Wellness control centre issues a termination command, the nearest drone to your location finds you and sends a kill signal directly to your Wellness Chip. That, in turn, triggers your pacemaker," he said, tapping his chest. "Instead of that blue thing doing what it normally does, which is regulate your heartbeat, it gives your heart a massive electric shock, and you die of a heart attack. Just like that," he said, snapping his fingers. "It's how they get rid of most people. The nearest drone takes you out…I mean, it takes just a few seconds…and then the drone calls a nearby disposal unit and, bang, you're gone. They wipe your records from the system, get rid of your body and, well, it's like you've never existed. You're just another termination."

Everyone was staring at the man intently, who looked up at the ceiling to gather his thoughts and then back down at his hands.

"Now, the important thing to remember here is that there are certain things that you can do in contravention of your Wellness Contract that will result in an immediate, automatic kill order. So, I don't know…let's say you introduce a certain chemical into your body. If it's serious enough, the Wellness Chip will pick it up and alert the nearest drone. And then the drone issues the termination order all by itself, without the need for the control centre to ever get involved. So basically the drone automatically tells your Wellness Chip to trigger your pacemaker, and you die."

He let his words sink in for a moment.

"Okay," said the well-built man. "I understand: You do something bad enough, you get killed straight away, by the drones."

"Exactly. It takes seconds, less, if there's a drone close by."

"Okay, but how can we use that to our advantage?"

The man shifted in his chair. "So, what we've been working on is something similar to geocasting. What we can do is, with a similar beamer…wait, hold on…" The man got up and rummaged around on a workbench next to a panel of computer screens, while the other people in the room glanced at each other. "Ah yes," he said after a few seconds, "here we go".

The man sat down and placed a small, rectangular plastic device, with two buttons on one side, on the table. "This is an early prototype, but it's basically an advanced version of the same beamer we use for geocasting. How it works is that you hold it next to your Wellness Chip and then you press this first button here." The man picked up the device and held his thumb over the top button. "What that does is allow the beamer to hack into your Wellness Chip and tell it you've contravened the Wellness Contract. Then, that information is automatically sent to the nearest drone. But, before the drone can issue the kill order, you press the second button and you cast the signal to your target." The man flicked his wrist as if he was throwing something in the direction of the man opposite.

"So…what?" The blond-haired man scratched his head. "The drone then kills whoever you want it to, whoever you've thrown the signal to, that is, rather than you?"

"Exactly. We use their system against them. Effectively, we issue a kill order against ourselves, and then we cast it to somebody else. So they die, instead of us. Instead of a geocast, you could think of it as a deathcast. But it's more than that. Because the system thinks it's killed us, not them, we get wiped from the system, not them."

"So we become invisible?"

"Yes. For a while, at least, until they figure out something strange has happened with their data. But, by then, we'll be long gone."

"Does that mean that we can only use it once, because we're no longer on their system?"

"No, not at all. You may no longer exist, but your Wellness Chip still has its serial number and, in effect, it's that that the drones are targeting, not you specifically. As I say, it's all automatic, so they're not checking with central records. So you can keep deathcasting, and the drones will keep on carrying out the kill orders.

"I have a question for you," asked the red-haired woman.

"Go on."

"Why can't we just hack into their Wellness Chip and

have the drone kill them directly. Why do we have to take the risk of a kill order being issued against us and then hoping we cast it in time to the target, before the drone terminates us?"

"It's a question of proximity. It's the same with the Care Chip. The beamer has to be right next to it to be able to hack into the Wellness Chip. You'd have to stand so close to the target that'd you'd never manage to do it unless they were already unconscious or dead."

"Okay, understood. Next question."

"Yes?"

"How far can we cast it? The Wellness contravention, I mean, from our Chip to the target's?"

"Ah, okay. I see what you're getting at. About 10 feet. I mean, that's the maximum, assuming there's no electrical interference and all of that sort of stuff."

"So, it's just for close combat, then."

"Well, basically, yes."

CHAPTER EIGHT

Several people in Wellness Department uniforms, including John, sat patiently waiting around a long, oblong table in a bright, white windowless meeting room.

One entire wall of the room was taken up with a touch-screen, showing the room number, all people currently present, the meeting agenda and links to related information, alongside urgent messages for attendees, the government news ticker, the current weather and other information. On a corner table were stacked Nutrimix packets and bottles of a clear liquid. A drone hovered around the camera dome in the middle of the ceiling.

The door to the meeting room slid open and Judith strode in and headed straight for the corner table. "Hello everyone," she said over her shoulder. "I'm sorry I'm late. I got a little held up at the gallery."

"Were they a difficult lot," someone asked.

Judith turned and glanced around the room to see who it was. "Yes, but I suppose they always are, more or less." She picked up a bottle of clear liquid. "What's this? Water?"

"No, it's a new drink we've been working on," a woman at

one end of the table said. "It's perfectly isotonic. You only need three bottles of this per day to stay completely hydrated. Water and all other drinks become unnecessary."

Unseen by Judith, a tall, older man in a different uniform from everyone else walked into the room and stood behind her. Everyone but Judith straightened up.

"Interesting," Judith said, turning the bottle in the light. "It seems a little more viscous than water. Shame they couldn't give it a colour."

"What would be the point of that," the tall man asked.

Judith jumped and swallowed nervously. "I'm sorry, Adam. I didn't see you there."

"I asked you a question: What would be the point of giving our perfect, clear drink a colour?"

Judith glanced uncomfortably around the room. All those sat around the table stared emptily back at her. "Um, well, to make it more appealing," she ventured.

"And why would it need to be 'more appealing'? As I said, it is perfect. Giving it a colour simply to satisfy outmoded and frankly childish notions of attractiveness would be a waste of effort and money. For it to be nutritious and beneficial to humankind should be enough to guarantee its appeal."

Judith laughed nervously. "I was just thinking it would be nice for it to be colourful. Everything else we have is grey."

Adam stared hard at Judith. "This is the most healthy drink that has ever been devised. Why would it need artifice for it to appeal to the people? People who, I might add, should be grateful to us for developing it on their behalf. There is no need for it to have a bright, primary colour."

"Sorry, I just meant…"

"I hardly think I need to remind you that we are on the brink of removing the burden of uncontrollable desire and the need for idle temptations from humanity. It would hardly be in keeping with that aim for us to give this liquid," Adam said, holding up a bottle, "a colour."

"No, of course not," Judith said uncomfortably.

"Well, if that is all, perhaps we can get started with the meeting."

Adam sat down at the head of the table and Judith found a place in the opposite corner. She tried to catch the eyes of the other people present, but no-one would look at her.

Once settled, Adam placed his hands flat on the table. "Welcome, everyone, to this Wellness Meeting." The wall screen announced the title of the meeting and brought the agenda to front of the screen. Reading his tablet, Adam said, "Perhaps, John, you could start us of by telling us about the latest developments in the Motivational Realignment project."

The doctor stood up and walked over to the screen. "Yes, thank you, Adam." John touched the first point on the agenda and the screen switched to a series of slides placed side-by-side and a live feed transmission from the laboratory, showing several people strapped into chairs, with metal discs over their eyes.

"As we discussed at the last meeting, the drive to recruit subjects to our Motivational Realignment study has been extremely successful and, since then, there have been several additional subjects enrolled over the past few days.

"As you may remember, participants in the study have transmitters placed over their eyes, held in place with corneal clips, to allow the introduction of various scenarios and visual patterns directly into the cortex. Combining brain scanning with data from the Care and Wellness chips, the aim initially was to identify key brain areas associated with motivation. This first, crucial part of the study has now been completed."

On the wall screen, a brain scan appeared, with a red area flashing in the frontal lobes.

"The second stage of the study is designed to determine whether, by introducing neuroactive chemicals into the body, we can modify the motivational areas of the subject's brain so that we eliminate that sadly all-too-human trait of seeking out self-destruction and danger."

A few people around the table nodded.

"So far, we have made great progress, and we successfully realigned two of the fifteen recruits who had been previously assigned to Permanent Correction, entirely removing any desire to do anything in contravention of the Wellness Contract. Of course, this is all very much at an early stage, and we have a long way to go before we can roll this out more widely, but the early signs from our initial data are very promising."

"What happened to the other thirteen subjects," someone asked.

"They died," the doctor said. "Unfortunately, the treatment was a little too effective, and they were unable to adjust to the changes that we brought about to their minds. However, with those two early successes, we have a firm platform to build on and refine our techniques."

The doctor paused and smiled. "The eventual aim of this project, of course, is to be able to, as it were, 'vaccinate' every child against desire and danger-seeking at the same time as they receive their Wellness Chip, so that this unhelpful aspect of human nature can be removed and every individual in our society can be set on the path to optimal Wellness at the earliest possible moment."

"Thank you, John." Adam stood up and the doctor went back to his chair. "As our colleague so clearly stated, out goal here is to remove any deviation from approved norms before they begin. We at the Wellness Department spend millions and millions every single year in Correcting people who do not pursue Wellness. And for what? They know they are supposed to place their health and wellbeing above all else. They know it's better for their own health and the health of our society. And yet they still don't pursue Wellness. Why not?"

Adam turned to the doctor. "Inform us, John."

The doctor went back to the screen and tapped, while Adam returned to his seat. The wall filled with images of neural connections and brain activity patterns.

"From our research, it seems that there are two strands of human motivation that are hampering our national Wellness goals. The first is the desire to be an individual. In other words, the desire to be different from other people, to stand out and be unique. The second is the desire for self-destruction, meaning the need to break the rules and to not follow any form of order or instruction. Of course, these two notions are related, and stem from the human—although not animal, it should be noted—need to be able to distinguish oneself from the crowd."

The doctor looked around the room. "Because of these desires, some people…not all, but a significant minority… will not pursue Wellness, no matter how much they know that they should. And what's worse is that they spread their desires, like a disease, to other people, to people who would ordinarily do the right thing and pursue Wellness. One could call them a cancer within our society."

Adam stood up, cutting in. "And, therefore, how much better for all of us, for every single person in society, if those desires were to be removed permanently, before they can do any harm to us." The table burst into even, rhythmic applause, while the doctor resumed his seat.

"Of course, we all know that there have been unenlightened souls in the Executive Committee who have questioned the need for our work," Adam continued. There was an audible groan of disapproval. "They point to the figures for 'traditional' crime, which have been at zero for decades, as a result of the introduction of the Care Chip and the ubiquitous drone presence."

Adam paced around the room.

"However, leaving aside those impressive statistics, it has been long recognised that people who fail to put their health and wellbeing first and remain productive for as long as possible are, in effect, committing a 'crime' against society. Of course, the Wellness Chip has gone a long way to drive that out, and the introduction of Nutrimix and the banning all other food stuffs have been enormously beneficial. But now, with the research led by John here," Adam gestured to the doctor, "we are entering a new paradigm, in which humanity will be able to shake off the yoke of unhelpful desires and everyone will be able to maximise their contribution to society."

Everyone around the room applauded.

Adam resumed his seat and checked his tablet. "Of course, while we are making progress for the future, we still have to deal with the present. Judith."

"Yes," she said, straightening up.

"How are the Wellness Correction visits going?"

"Yes, thank you." Judith stood up and cleared her throat. "Since our last meeting, there have been a number of visits to the Wellness Correction Gallery, so that the friends and family of people assigned to Permanent Correction can witness our work in action, so to speak, and understand why they should ensure that they and those around them keep to the Wellness Contract."

Judith tapped the wall screen and a live feed transmitted from the gallery overlooking the laboratory flashed up.

"We have been able to give viewers in the gallery the benefit of seeing their loved ones in the moment of their final, Permanent, Correction. As a part of that process, John's team have also been able to mine subjects' memories and thoughts, which has led, in some cases, to the breaking of smuggling rings and the identification of other transgressors of the Wellness Contract." Judith looked around the room. "We have another visit this afternoon, so I'll update you on that and the other visits at the next meeting," she said, before quickly resuming her seat.

"Thank you, Judith," Adam said casually, while reading his tablet. "However, I would like to note that not all of your Wellness Correction visits have gone according to plan, have they?"

Adam looked up and stared at Judith.

"No, Adam," she said quietly.

"There have been a number of situations of late in which the relatives have had quite violent and disruptive emotional reactions to seeing their loved ones being Corrected, despite it being in their best interests."

"Yes, there have."

"I'm sure you appreciate that this cannot continue."

"No, of course not."

"You must retain control of the visits at all times. It is of paramount importance for the Wellness of all present."

"Yes, Adam. Thank you."

Adam held Judith's gaze. "Failure in the future may suggest that you are not suitable for this privileged post. In which case, we would have to reassess your future here at the Department."

Judith swallowed. "I understand. Thank you."

They started at each other for a moment.

"That will be all, everyone," Adam said, looking around. "Thank you for your attention."

Everyone got up and filed out of the room, while Adam stayed behind, checking his tablet.

CHAPTER NINE

ON ONE SIDE OF THE GLASS-WALLED LOBBY OF THE WELLNESS
Department was a large reception desk, several doors and a
bank of lifts, with everything in bright, glossy white plastic.
Several heavily armed guards in face marks patrolled around
the edge of the lobby, while two drones circled around a
large camera dome in the centre of the ceiling.

Outside, it was grey and rainy, and passers-by had their
head down as they walked.

A group of visitors, all dressed in standard-issue
uniforms, were waiting patiently, drying out after the rain.
Although they appeared calm and placid, they stood together
in a small circle, looking out at the rest of the room. One or
two whispered among themselves as they waited. Everyone
tried to avoid eye contact.

The last to join the group were Maggie and Poppy, who
arrived in a rush from the noisy outside world. As they
walked in, their presence was registered on a large wall
screen over the reception desk, which told them to join the
rest of the group waiting to start the visit.

The both quietly, surreptitiously joined the back of the group. A woman with shoulder-length red hair and a man with dark hair and glasses glanced at the newcomers and Maggie smiled back nervously. She bent down and set to work putting Poppy's hair, which had come undone on the journey, back into bunches.

Maggie had just finished and straightened up when Judith strode out of a side door and straight over to the group. Despite Judith's broad smile, the entire group stiffened.

"Good afternoon, everyone," she said brightly. "Welcome to the Wellness Department, and thank you for coming; some of you at short notice, I know." Judith glanced around the group, and then checked her tablet. "I see that everyone is here. So, if you'd like to follow me…"

She turned towards the lifts, and the group quietly formed two lines and walked at an even pace behind her. At the lifts, she stopped and a panel on the wall displayed a message:

Lift called for Judith

The group stood patiently behind her. Curious to see where they were going, Poppy tried to step out of the line, but Maggie pulled her back.

The lift door opened to reveal a bright, white, seamless space. Judith stood aside to usher everyone in. "We should all be able to fit in one lift, I think," she said brightly. The visitors marched in quietly. As Poppy arrived at the lift door, Judith looked down. "Watch your step, little one."

Poppy looked up at Judith suspiciously. Maggie placed her hands on her daughters shoulders. "Sorry, she's very young."

"Not at all," Judith said, looking up. "She's a very pretty child. What's her name?"

"Poppy."

Judith got down on her haunches. "Hello Poppy. Now, mind your step when you get in, and make sure you stay with you mother, okay?"

"Okay," the girl said and stepped carefully over the gap between the lift and the floor.

Judith stood up. "Everybody in," she asked. No-one replied. "Good," she said, getting into the lift and pressing a button. The doors slid silently shut and, with hardly a jolt, the lift descended. A counter above the door slowly ticked down: G, B, -1, -2, -3, -4.

The lift slowed to a standstill.

"Here we are ladies and gentlemen…and little girls." Judith smiled down at Poppy, who was holding onto her mother's leg.

The lift doors opened and the group slowly filed out of the lift and into a white, bright windowless room with a reception desk at one end and two large, airtight doors flanking the reception desk. On one wall was a large piece of art, which shimmered and pulsated with bright, shifting colours. A drone hovered around the camera dome in the middle of the ceiling, while a heavily armed, masked guard paced up and down.

While the group formed two single files along the wall opposite the art, Judith walked over to the reception desk. "Hello David. I've brought the next group of visitors for you."

David consulted the tablet screen embedded in his desk.

"Are you ready for us," Judith asked. "Or should we hang around for a few minutes?"

"It looks like they're still getting ready for you," David said. "It should only be a short while. I'll let you know when they're done."

Judith tapped the desk with her finger. "Okay, I'll show them our latest piece of art, in that case." She walked back the group and cleared her throat. They turned to face her as one. "We have a few minutes before we go into the gallery, so I thought I'd draw your attention to this rather fine example of Academy art."

She stepped over to the shimmering, evolving picture and the group silently gathered in front of it. "It's lovely, isn't it?"

The group murmured in agreement. One of the visitors standing near the front spoke up. "How do they get it to have such rich colours? It has much more depth than most I've seen."

Judith cleared her throat. "Well, as with all Academy art, the colours were chosen based on complex algorithms and metrics, to guide your mood to its optimum state for this environment." A couple of the visitors nodded in appreciation. "However, seeing as we are in the Wellness Department and, given the importance of the work that we do here, no expense has been spared in terms of the choice of materials and in the quality of the finish, which, as you can see..." Judith swept her hand over the surface, "...is second to none."

Several members of the group leaned in to appreciate it better, while Maggie picked up Poppy so that she could get a closer look.

Judith continued, "The supercomputer that produces these artworks processes data on thousands and thousands of parameters not only to calculate the ideal state of mind we want a visitor to the Wellness Department to be in when they come here, but also to match that to predetermined colour palettes and patterns."

"The computer's task is then to create the most evocative and stimulating work possible," Judith said, adding, "I'm sure you'll agree that it has been most successful in its aim."

She waved her hand over a panel on the wall. The ambient light in the white corridor lowered and the picture shimmered into life, generating a complex and strangely beautiful pattern of colours and light that swirled and pulsated across the frame. The group drifted into a trance. Their breathing became regular and the expressions fell away from their faces.

Only Poppy, who had gone back to holding onto her mother's leg, did not look at the picture but glanced around the room. Maggie had been stroking her hair but, as the effect of the picture took hold, her hand fell by her side.

Eventually, the swirling, shimmering pattern of colour and light slowed and the ambient light of the room increased. Judith gazed with satisfaction at the quiet and subdued group.

"They're ready for you now," David said.

Judith turned and smiled at him. "Thank you." Addressing the group, she said, "If you'd like to follow me."

Judith walked over to one of the airtight doors by the reception desk. In complete silence and staring straight ahead, the group lined up behind her. She punched a code into a panel and pulled open the door. The group slowly filed through the door and into a long, bare, white corridor. Only Poppy glanced back at the room as she disappeared from view.

Partway along the corridor, a metal frame running across the floor, up the walls and across the ceiling switched on as the group approached. A blue light ran continuously along its length, flashing each time one of the group passed.

As Maggie guided Poppy through the scanner, gently pushing her from behind, an alarm sounded and red lights flashed in the ceiling. Maggie looked horrified and the whole group stared disapprovingly, while Poppy grabbed hold of her mother in fright. Judith calmly walked over to a control panel in the wall and switched off the alarm. She then knelt down in front of Poppy and smiled broadly.

"Don't worry, Poppy," she said. "I'm sure it's nothing serious."

She checked around her face. "Ah, I think it might be this," she said, reaching over and pulling a metal clip out of her hair. "There we go. No metal objects down here, I'm afraid. They should have told you in reception, but it doesn't matter."

Judith stood up and ushered Poppy forward. "Do you want to try again?"

Poppy stepped through the scanner, but no alarm sounded this time.

Maggie sighed with relief. "Thank you," she said to Judith.

"That's okay. I'll hang onto it until we're done, and then you can have it back."

Maggie frowned. "But won't it set the alarms off?"

"No, I'm authorised to carry metal objects," she said, and pocketed the clip.

Further along the white corridor, Academy art shimmered and glowed as they passed, returning the visitors to their trance-like state. While the rest of the group were calm, Poppy looked around nervously. She slipped her hand into Maggie's and squeezed her mother's fingers. But Maggie did not respond, and her arms hung limply by her side.

They reached a heavy, reinforced door, with a small glass observation window. Judith punched a code into a panel and, after a series of clicks, the door withdrew slowly into the wall. The visitors filed two-by-two into the viewing gallery over the laboratory. At either end stood heavily armed guards in masks, while a drone circled around a camera dome in the middle of the room. In front of the thick, reinforced glass wall overlooking the laboratory stood a pedestal adorned with a large red button. The group aligned themselves in front of the glass wall and gazed down in silence at the rows of chairs arranged in a semi-circle in front of the gallery, all of which were filled. Wellness Department workers moved in-between the chairs, taking notes on their tablets and checking the occupants, all of whom had metal discs attached to heavy cables fixed over their eyes. Occasional adjustments were made and individual subjects discussed, although it was impossible to hear what they said. From their vantage point, it seemed to the visitors as if each occupant was asleep, perhaps dreaming. Some appeared even to be smiling.

Judith walked over to the pedestal and turned to face the visitors, who turned as one to look at her. She cleared her throat. "Welcome, everyone, to the Wellness Correction Gallery. I imagine that the majority of you have some idea what you are seeing and why you are here. It is also just as likely, however, that you are not aware of the full range of work that we do here at the Wellness Department, and its importance in maintaining the stability and prosperity of our society."

Judith glanced around the room. Everyone was attentive to her words, but their expressions were passive, almost empty. Only Poppy was not concentrating on what she said, and started to fidget.

"We, as individuals, as a people and a nation, stand on the brink of greatness. Indeed, we stand on the brink of achieving all that our visionary forefathers could possibly have dreamt for us. After all, we have almost eliminated all disease and made our lives productive and useful both to ourselves and society. Moreover, we have learned what it takes to achieve perfect Wellness and how to guide ourselves to that state."

Judith glanced down at the room below.

"And yet, despite the great gifts that our government

bestows upon us, and amazing as this may seem, it appears that not everyone is as willing to make the small efforts required of us to reach our personal and collective goals. These people we see below us," she said, gesturing down to the chairs, "are either unwilling or unable to do that."

In unison, everyone turned their gaze from Judith to the laboratory below. Curious, Poppy let go of her mother's hand. She pushed between the legs of the group and made her way to the front. At the glass wall, she placed her palms on the cold surface and stared down into the laboratory, her breath forming semi-circles of condensation on the glass.

"Of course, I need not remind any of you that each and every one of us, including those people down there in the laboratory, have signed the Pledge of Perpetual Allegiance and the Wellness Contract. Everyone of us. Yet, tine and again, those people have failed us, and themselves. Time and again, they have contravened their Wellness Contract and jeopardised us all. And time and again, they have been warned and they have been Corrected, but still they carry on."

Poppy took in the machines, the workers in their uniforms, and the people strapped into the chairs, with metal discs over their eyes.

"We therefore cannot waste our valuable, precious resources on people who are not willing to follow something they have already agreed to, who are not willing to value their own Wellness and dedicate themselves to our society. How could we justify allowing that to continue? These people, who have failed time and time again," she empha-sised, "need to be Corrected. Permanently."

As Judith finished speaking, the gallery was filled with an ear-piercing scream that made everyone snap out of their reverie. The guards stepped forward and snapped off the safety catch on their weapons. Everyone turned and stared at

Poppy, who was leaning with her back against the glass with a look of abject horror on her face. She stared up at Maggie, whose passive expression crumbled at her daughter's anguish. The young girl pointed at one of the chairs in the laboratory. "It's daddy. Daddy's down there."

CHAPTER TEN

A young man in a military uniform stared at a monitoring screen showing a live feed from the gallery. He frowned and checked his tablet. When he glanced back at the screen, Judith was staring up at him.

Adam walked up behind the young man and looked over his shoulder. "What's happening down there? I heard an alarm go off."

The guard shifted in his seat. "Yes, sir. It was in the gallery, just now. The audio monitors picked up a scream and switched my monitor."

"Do we know what's going on?"

"Well, if we check here…" the guard said, scrolling back the live feed. "Ah yes, this must be it."

The monitor screen showed Poppy leaning against the glass wall of the gallery and staring down into the laboratory. She screamed and turned away. Subtitles on the bottom of the screen read:

IT IS DADDY. DADDY IS DOWN THERE.

"It seems she must have recognised her father in the Correction Lab," the young man said, turning to look up at Adam.

Adam stared at the monitor, narrowing his eyes. "Do we know any more? Who is the girl? Who is she with?"

"Let's see," the young man said. He checked his tablet and the monitor switched to a split screen, with Maggie's file on one side and Poppy's on the other. "That's…Maggie, she's the mother of the girl, who's called…Poppy."

"And?"

As the screen ran more and more information, the guard continued, "They were both invited to the gallery, it says, because Maggie's husband, Patrick, was arrested last week after a tip-off about alcohol consumption in the dead zone. It turns out that he's been arrested numerous times for Wellness contraventions, and a download of his brain data revealed he's part of a terrorist organisation that's behind some of the recent attacks, although we didn't find out anything about who else is in the cell or any future strikes. He was then assigned to the Motivational Realignment study, in advance of being Permanently Corrected, which is set for today."

"Show me Maggie, now, in the gallery."

The young man switched back to the live feed.

"Hmm, she looks agitated," Adam said. "I wonder if she'll crack."

The two men watched as Judith ordered the group back into line and then pressed a button in the wall. The lights dimmed and the glass wall turned into a swirling, shimmering pattern of rich, evocative colours.

"Good, she's pacifying them."

The young man checked his tablet. "Their heart rate is dropping already. It looks like it's working."

"All right," Adam said. "Let it play, but if things start getting out of hand again, Correct them all. Okay?"

The young man turned to Adam. "Everyone, sir? Including Judith?"

"Yes, including Judith. I warned her earlier today. There is no room for error in the Wellness Department."

"Yes, sir," the young man said, returning to the monitor.

Adam straightened up and walked away.

IN THE GALLERY, ambient noise emanated from unseen speakers, pulsating and evolving with the patterns on the glass wall. The faces of the visitors were calm and passive.

Judith switched off the images and the ambient noise slowly faded away. The drone, which had been poised and still, returned to circling around the camera dome. She glanced across at the guards and shook her head. They slowly stepped back and re-engaged the safety catches on their guns, lowering the muzzles.

She then looked down at Poppy, who had tears streaming down her face. The young girl's eyes darted from person to person, searching for a connection. Eventually, she realised that Judith was gazing at her and she caught her eye. Judith smiled.

"Daddy is down there," Poppy wailed, pointing to the laboratory below. "Mummy," she cried. She ran to Maggie but, before she could get there, Judith stepped forward and swept her up into her arms.

"I want my mummy," Poppy shouted, hitting Judith with her fists, her face red and contorted.

"Poppy," Judith barked and squeezed the girl hard. Poppy stopped shouting and stared fearfully into Judith's face. "Poppy, do you know what's happening here?"

The young girl looked into the woman's eyes and nodded.

Judith stared back at her intently, noticing the small flecks of brown around the young girl's pupils.

"Daddy is going to be Corrected," Poppy said quietly.

"Yes, that's right, Poppy. But do you know why?"

Poppy shook her head and began to cry again, the tears rolling down her face.

Still holding her tight in her arms, Judith turned to face the laboratory below.

"Poppy, can you point out your daddy for me?"

The young girl searched around the room and then pointed at a chair towards the middle. "He's there."

Judith adjusted her arm. "He looks peaceful, doesn't he?" Poppy nodded, still gazing down at her father. "He is peaceful, Poppy, down there. He's practically asleep. He hardly knows where he is." Judith reflected. "Maybe he thinks his back in your house in the city, or maybe he's back in the house where he lived as a child. Who knows? But you can be sure of one thing, and that's that your father isn't suffering."

Poppy wiped her face and swallowed.

"Did you know that everyone who's come here today knows someone who's down there in that room," Judith asked. Poppy shook her head. "Everyone is her because a relative or someone close to them needs to be Corrected, just like your father. And the important thing for you to realise, Poppy, is that we never Correct anyone unless we absolutely have to. Do you understand?"

Poppy searched Judith's face.

"Do you remember the lessons you learned in your Dutiful Citizen and Wellness classes," she asked. Poppy nodded slowly. "And do you remember why we have to Correct people? After all, you signed your Wellness Contract and had your chip fitted only this morning. I'm sure your teacher has told you several times that every one of us has to pursue Wellness, not only for our own health but for the health of society." Judith adjusted her arm. "Do you remember that, Poppy?"

"Yes."

"Good, because your father signed that Contract too. Just like you did. But I'm sorry to say that he broke his Contract. Many times. And, now, he needs to be Corrected."

"Why?"

"Look, I don't know what your father did in particular, Poppy, but I do know that people are Corrected for all sorts of reasons, mostly for having undesirable habits, like smoking or drinking alcohol or eating unhealthy food, or for not getting the right amount of sleep or exercise, for being overweight, or for taking risks…the list goes on." Judith sighed. "You know, we've known for a long time what makes us well, what makes us more productive, what's good for us, and we have also known for a long time that those things are not only good for us as individuals but also for society as a whole, because society is nothing without its people."

"The problem we had in the past was we thought that 'free will' was more important than collective responsibility. We thought that a person's right to choose how to live their life and how to look after their body and mind was more important than what they did with it." Judith shook her head and laughed. "But how can that be right, when a smoker puts themselves at risk of serious, long-term illness that stops them working, and we have to pay for their care, year after year? How can that be right when someone who drinks alcohol places themselves at risk of accidents and disease, and experiences reductions in productivity and changes in their behaviour that run counter to everything that our society stands for?"

Judith smiled. "The big breakthrough was when we realised that there is no such thing as the sanctity of human life when that life is not dedicated to helping society as a whole. It was then that we saw that Correction was not just crucial to ensure that individuals behaved as they themselves had pledged to do, but was a moral imperative in order to safeguard us all."

Poppy frowned.

"Your father is down there, Poppy, because he won't pursue his own Wellness. We can't have that. We paid for his education, for his nourishment. We provided him with a job and a home, and guaranteed him a living wage. We assigned him a wife and gave him a human embryo to raise as his own." Judith looked into Poppy's eyes. "We gave him you."

"And, Poppy, he took everything we gave to him, gladly, and all we asked in return was that he lived in the best possible way to guarantee his productivity and contribution to our society. You, me, everyone in this room…We all have a stake in each other's Wellness, including your father's. So, by extension, we have a stake in his efforts to maintain his Wellness. In other words, we own him—you, me and everyone here. We own him and his body, and so his duty to all of us is to protect himself and his body."

"Look at your father, Poppy." They both looked down into the laboratory. "Whatever he's done, your father has broken his Pledge to society, as has every single other person down there. They have all broken their pledges. So, we have to Correct them. Permanently. It's the only way we can help them, and us. It's for the best."

Judith turned back to Poppy. "Have you understood what I've said?"

"Yes," the girl replied quietly.

"Then would you like to help me?" Poppy nodded, and Judith, adjusting her arm, walked over to the pedestal with the large red button. "All you have to do, sweetheart, is press that red button. Can you see it?"

Poppy reached out with her small, delicate hands, and

Judith bent down so that the young girl could reach the button. Poppy's hand hovered over the smooth, plastic surface. "Go on," Judith said, "press it."

But before Poppy could push the button, Judith convulsed violently and, dropping Poppy, fell to the floor. An alarm sounded and the lights in the room flashed red. Pulling herself free, Poppy looked up to see one of the visitors pressing a small plastic device to his wrist and then flicking it towards a guard, who immediately fell dead.

Overhead, the drone zipped back and forth, dipping down towards each of the visitors in turn, who immediately fell dead. Someone screamed, "The drone," and a tall, blond-haired man jumped over to the fallen guard, grabbing his gun and blasting it out of the air, before turning and shooting the other guard, who was grappling with one of the visitors.

Down below, in the flashing, alarm-filled darkness of the laboratory, the assistant was, strap-by-strap, disconnecting Patrick from his chair. John lay dead on the floor beside him, and a laboratory worker with close-cropped hair and an angular face had taken a gun and was shooting anyone or anything that came into view.

Poppy watched as her father was freed, and then the metal discs carefully removed from his eyes. She looked away in fright when she saw the blood running down his face and his wrenched-open eye sockets.

When she could bring herself to turn back, she saw he was being dragged towards the door of the laboratory by two men, who were shooting and neutralising the guards and drones as they poured in from the opposite end of the laboratory.

A hand grabbed her roughly and she was hoisted onto the shoulders of a well-built man with a shaved head.

"Just shoot it," someone shouted. There was a loud blast and Poppy pulled herself around to see the gallery door slowly sliding open. Without waiting to see what was on the other side, two visitors were hacking their Wellness Chips in readiness, while two others, armed with the guards' guns, trained their weapons on the door. Maggie and the visitor gripping Poppy to his shoulder, waited behind, counting down the eternal seconds.

As the soon as the door slid back far enough the visitors flicked their deathcasters, managing to catch two guards as they pushed into the gallery. The other two opened fire, killing two more guards, while the first two rearmed their Wellness Chips.

The door now fully open, the guards pushed further in, managing to shoot the deathcaster out of the hand of a visitor before she could throw the kill order, and she died as soon as another drone flew in through the door.

The visitors carried on fighting, using the armour taken from the dead guards to protect themselves as they pushed towards the door and out into the corridor. The man holding Poppy shot several guards, while ordering Maggie to use him as cover. She held back a few paces, afraid and panicking from the wail of the alarm and the endless ricochet of gunfire.

The man clambered over the fallen guards, and Poppy clawed back to her mother, fear in her eyes. "Mummy, come, please," she cried, stretching her fingers out across the space between them. Maggie, thrusting her hand towards her daughter, stumbled and fell.

The man broke free from the pile of bodies and ran down the corridor, taking Poppy further and further away from her mother. A drone flew past them and towards her mother, dipping as it approached. The young girl screamed.

CUT OUT AND KEEP

CHAPTER ONE

IN THE WARM EMBRACE OF A LATE SUMMER EVENING, A COUPLE in their late twenties walked arm-in-arm through the leafy back streets of a well-heeled part of Islington.

She was radiant, brimming with hope that this quietly confident man might just be the one to accompany her in the fulfilment of her romantic dreams. As they walked, she leant on his arm and swung out a leg from time to time, her vintage silk dress slipping back to reveal the shining grace of her form. She laughed brightly with each of his tasteful pleasantries, her voice echoing into the red and yellow sky, and her eyes shone with delight at their shared, easy comfort.

They passed converted churches, chic local pubs and exclusive galleries, nestling between launderettes and hardware stores, all framed by the classical Georgian symmetry of the well-kept houses. The light within the couple lent a glow to their surroundings that mixed enchantingly with the gold of the falling sun.

Outside a corner shop, Jack was folding and tidying a pile of empty cardboard boxes. Stopping to stretch his back, he delighted in the young woman as the couple approached. He had seen her pass by many times before and noted her elegant charm, but she never as seemed ravishing and luminescent as on that evening. He watched her, enraptured, like a man seeing beauty for the first time.

They young couple walked right past the shop, oblivious to the world, lost as they were in the infinite self-reference of their growing intimacy. As a consequence, the woman didn't notice how Jack gazed at her intently, tracing her every gesture and movement with his eyes.

As they walked further up the street, Jack turned back to his work, resigned to letting go of the vision that had so entranced him.

A few yards on, the woman stopped and turned, hesitating before walking back towards the shop. Jack noticed all of this out of the corner of his eye with a growing sense of nervousness, but he hardly dared acknowledge that it was happening. It was only when she was standing right next to him and he could see the perfect glow of her skin so close to him that he found the courage to look up.

He smiled nervously.

"Hi," she said in a gentle, warm voice. "You work here, right?"

"Um, yes," the young man said timidly, straightening up and dusting his hands on his old jeans. "Every day."

"Great," she said. Her smile pierced his soul and elevated him a little closer to the vespertine sky. "Could you do me a favour?"

"Yes, anything you want, anything at all," he said quickly, his voice catching in his throat. "What can I do for you?" he added in a more serious tone.

She gestured at the pile of boxes by his feet. "Actually, I need some of these. I'm moving out in a couple of weeks."

"Oh," Jack said, disappointed.

"So, I need to pack up my stuff, and these'd be perfect. Do you think you could let save me some?"

"Um, yes, no problem. How many do you want?"

"Oh, I don't know...As many as you can get? I need to put most of my stuff in storage. My boyfriend here," she looked over her shoulder at her companion, who loitered discreetly by a tree, "has loads of stuff already, and he's says it's all better than mine." She laughed and placed her hand on Jack's arm.

The young man followed the arc of her movement, watching almost in slow motion, and his heart chimed to the delicate grip of her fingers through his thin jacket. "Oh," he said, his mind a whirl of emotions.

"So, I need a lot of boxes," she said, taking her hand away again.

"When do you need them by," he asked, recovering himself. "We've got a delivery coming tomorrow morning, so I can keep all the boxes from that for you, if you want. We should be done with unpacking everything and have them all ready for you by tomorrow evening?"

Her eyes widened with delight. "That'd be amazing. Thank you. You've saved my life."

Jack smiled and looked away. "When will you come for them," he asked shyly, unable to look directly at her smile.

"Um, Friday would perfect. Is that okay for you?"

"Of course. I'll keep them in the back and bring them out here when you need them."

"Thank you so much, you are so very kind," she said, smiling indulgently. With that, she skipped over to her beau, and they linked arms and walked away. Jack stood watching them in silence and, when she turned back and waved, he melted.

Sighing and his heart filled with desire, Jack went back to sorting out the boxes to take them to the back of the shop.

When he looked up, he saw Vince leaning on the doorframe and smirking. Jack tried to ignore him and went back to the pile of flattened boxes.

"Of course it's okay, my pretty lady," Vince said in a mocking voice. "Anything you want, pretty lady. Anything at all."

"Leave me alone," Jack said quietly.

Vince laughed to himself and watched Jack working. The light was fading. The streetlamp over their heads switched on for the evening. "Are you actually going to keep the boxes for her?"

Jack straightened up and frowned. "Yes, of course. Why not?"

"But you do know that she's never going to come back and collect them, right?"

"Yes she will," Jack said indignantly. "She said so. Why wouldn't she?"

"She'll forget she asked you and get them from somewhere else. Or her boyfriend will find some for her because he doesn't want her to talk to you."

"That's not true. She'll be back, and I'll have all the boxes she needs, ready and waiting for her."

Vince laughed to himself as he pushed off the doorframe and walked back into the shop. "We'll see, kid." Jack shook his head and pulled a face behind Vince's back.

CHAPTER TWO

EARLY NEXT MORNING, JACK TOOK THE DELIVERY, PILING UP all the boxes outside the shop. It was much colder, and the young professionals rushing to work sported thick, warm clothes. The cyclists battled against the harsh wind whipping up dust and dropped food cartons, and it all seemed a million years since the light summer evening only the day before.

Jack dallied a while on the step of the shop before taking in the boxes, wondering whether he would be able to recognise her in her autumnal clothes, even if she happened to pass by at that moment. He was woken from his reverie by a customer pushing past to buy a packet of cigarettes. Realising he was being silly, he carried the boxes through to the storeroom at the back of the shop.

Hours later, Jack was stacking the shelves, glancing along the narrow aisles stuffed from floor to ceiling from time to time to see if a customer appeared and needed to pass. Lost in his thoughts, he pulled aside a tin and, there, on the other side of the shelf, looking straight at him, was her. She was smiling at him, beaming gloriously.

Shocked, Jack stepped back and put his foot into box of

noodles, smashing several packets and nearly falling into a stack of toilet paper. Cursing, he pulled himself up and rushed back into the gap in the shelves were he had seen her. But there was no-one there. Nothing. Just the cat food piled up on the shelf opposite. Jack ran around to the other aisle but it was empty. Puzzled, he went back to the box of noodles. A woman walked in and Jack looked up, desperate for it be her. But it was just another customer, buying some chewing gum.

All the while, Vince watched Jack's antics on the CCTV screen by the till and chuckled to himself.

That evening, Jack flicked on the brutal neon strip light of the storeroom. On the floor in front of him lay a large pile of carefully folded cardboard boxes. Sighing, Jack dropped two more boxes on top of the pile. He switched off the light and closed the door carefully behind him.

CHAPTER THREE

Several days later, Jack was outside the shop, folding up boxes from another delivery, wrapped up warm against the cold. All the while, he looked up and down the street.

"When did she say she'd be back," Vince asked as he leaned against the doorframe.

"Friday," Jack said sadly.

"I told you she wouldn't come back."

"But it's only Monday," Jack protested. "Maybe she was busy on Friday. Maybe she went away for the weekend."

"Pah," Vince said, laughing. "Dream on, kid."

Placing the last folded box on top of the pile, Jack said: "She said she needs them to move. She'll be back, for sure."

"We'll see."

Two days later, just after the last pub had closed, Vince and Jack were closing up for the night, Jack tidying the shelves while Vince counted the money in the till.

"Are you still thinking about that woman," Vince asked.

"What woman," Jack shot back defensively.

"You know exactly who I mean."

Jack sighed. "Yeah, maybe I am."

"You're going to have to accept it, kid. She's never coming back. Why don't you just get rid of those boxes, eh?"

"She'll come, I know it," Jack said earnestly. "And I'm keeping every one of those boxes until she does. Anyway, they're not taking up much space, and the storeroom is half empty."

"Suit yourself, Jack, but it was two weeks ago when she asked. She must've moved out by now."

Jack glanced over to the storeroom. "She won't forget," he said quietly to himself. "She'll come back."

The two men lapsed into silence, returning to their tasks.

"I know what'll take your mind off her," Vince called out.

"What's that," Jack asked, as he straightened out the piles of toilet paper and separated out the misplaced kitchen rolls.

"Stocktaking. It always helps me forget my problems."

"Oh great," Jack said wearily. "Just what I need."

'I'm telling you, kid. Whenever your auntie used to get on my nerves, which was a lot when we were younger, I used to come down here and forget all about it with a ledger and a nice, long stock-take. Why don't you give it a try?"

Jack stared at Vince as if he was mad.

"Look, forget about that woman, Jack," Vince said. "Put your mind into something else, something real," he added, gesturing around the shop. Jack sighed and rolled his eyes.

CHAPTER FOUR

Jack switched on the neon light in the store room and stared sadly at the pile of boxes. After a moment lost in contemplation, he went to leave but decided to rearrange the boxes and tidy them up. As he was finishing, he heard a shout from Vince. "Hurry up in there, we've got customers waiting."

"Okay," Jack said, and switched off the light.

That evening, a young couple walked past the shop while Jack was sweeping up outside. They were arm-in-arm and laughed loudly as he told her a story. Jack watched them wistfully and sighed. Then he had a flash of inspiration. He quickly finished sweeping up, put back the brush and went to the storeroom.

Once the neon light had stopped flickering, he stared at the pile of boxes, scratching his stubble, and then glanced back at the shop. There were no customers, and everything was quiet. "Why didn't you come back," Jack asked the boxes in a quiet voice.

"What are you doing back there," Vince called from the till.

"Nothing, nothing," Jack shouted, and pushed the store-room door shut. He upended an old plastic crate and sat down on it, composing himself in front of the pile of boxes. "Why didn't you come back," he asked again.

He sighed heavily. "No, this isn't right."

Jack got up and rummaged around on one of the shelves. Eventually, he found a pair of old, rusty scissors and set to work on the boxes, cutting out shapes and inspecting them. After several false starts, he arranged the best pieces into the shape of a woman and carefully stapled them together. He then found a marker pen and drew on a face and some hair, trying to make it as close as possible to the woman, before standing back to admire his handiwork. "That's better," he said.

He sat back down on the crate and settled himself. "I was hoping you would come back, you know." He paused. "I'd love you better than that other man. I'm sure of it. He don't deserve you."

Jack looked at the felt-tip face, which stared blankly back at him.

"You should've got to know me. I'm a nice guy, and I can be kind. I'd have bought you flowers and that, and I'd've taken you out to dinner."

Jack reflected. "All those times you came by the shop...I thought you'd've noticed me at least once. But I guess not," he added sadly. He laughed to himself. "I bet you smile like that for everybody."

Jack turned to check the door was still shut and that Vince wasn't standing behind him, arms folded and smirking.

"It's rubbish working here, you know," Jack said conspiratorially. "But I have to. I've been working here since I was a kid. It's my uncle's shop, and he needs me. Him and my auntie couldn't have kids of their own, so I had to help out here. Anyway, I didn't do so well at school, so I didn't have much choice, know what I mean?"

Jack shifted on his crate. "But I want to do other things, you know. I want to travel, and see the world." He paused. "At one point, I wanted to be a graphic designer, but it didn't work out." He brightened up. "And I want to get married one day. Not to one of them girls down the pub or that club we always go to on a Friday night. I mean someone really nice, who I'd love." Jack stared at the box face. "But maybe that's silly…"

Before he could continue, he heard Vince shouting: "Are you going to be in there all night or are you going to help me out here. We've got customers, you know."

"Sorry," he called back, "I'll be out in a sec." He quickly tidied away the crate and buried his cardboard lady under the rest of the boxes. Then he stood in the middle of the room and frowned, lost in thought, before switching off the light and slamming the door shut behind him.

CHAPTER FIVE

Over the next few weeks, Jack spent longer and longer in the storeroom, talking to his cardboard lady and unburdening himself of all the feelings he'd never had the opportunity to express before. A brightness came over him, and he began to open up and interact more with the customers, greeting them with a smile and remembering details of their lives.

One day, Vince watched Jack while he was walking through the shop, whistling. "Are you all right, kid," Vince asked as the young man passed.

Jack, who was carrying a pile of empty boxes, stopped and smiled. "Yes, why?"

"You seem different."

"Oh yes? How so?"

"I don't know." Vince shrugged. "Just, you seem...happy."

"What's wrong with that," Jack asked, surprised.

"No, no, nothing," Vince said quickly. "It's just that, well, I don't think I've ever seen you happy before."

"Really? Never?"

"Yeah, you know. You've always been a bit mopey."

Jack thought for a moment. "Fair enough, I suppose I was," he said and started walking on.

Vince cleared his throat. "I've noticed you're spending a lot of time in the store room," the older man said.

Jack froze. "It's nothing. I'm just working on something," he said quickly and took the boxes outside. He placed them in a pile next to the bin, ready for the recycling van to take them away, and looked up and down the street. A couple were walking past on the other side of the road. As he watched them talking happily and laughing together, he had a dawning realisation and marched back through the shop, all the while watched by Vince.

In the storeroom, he carefully closed the door behind him, dragged over the upturned crate and sat down heavily. He tilted his head and gazed at the box woman, who stared blankly back at him. "I realised something just now, box lady," Jack said. "When I made you, I was lonely and I needed someone to talk to."

He sighed. "And I talked to you a lot, didn't I."

Jack paused and checked that Vince hadn't followed him unseen into the storeroom. "But you know what? Thanks to you, I feel so much better about myself now. I'm like a new person. I hardly recognise myself in the mirror," he enthused.

"But..." Jack looked down at the floor and back up at the felt-tip face. "It's hard for me to say this, but I think I need to find a real person to talk to, if you know what I mean."

He smiled awkwardly. "I'm sorry. It's not you, you know. It's me. I just don't think that me coming here everyday to talk to you is helping me any more." He hesitated. "I mean, it did help me, a lot. But, now, I think it's kind-of holding me back. Know what I mean? I think that just talking to you about my feelings is stopping me from growing, as a person. I need to speak to other people, to get their...point of view.

It's no good just hearing my own opinion on things all the time."

Jack sighed. "I'm sorry to say this but I think, tomorrow, I'm going to have to put you in the recycling." He thought for a moment. "But I'll never forget you, you know, and everything that you've done for me. Never."

Jack stared for a while at the cardboard lady, and her impassive expression. Eventually, he got up and, after one last glance and a deep sigh, turned and opened the storeroom door.

But just as he was about to cross the threshold and switch off the light, he heard a small voice.

"Don't go. I think I love you."

Jack stopped, and smiled.

STATIONS OF THE SOUL

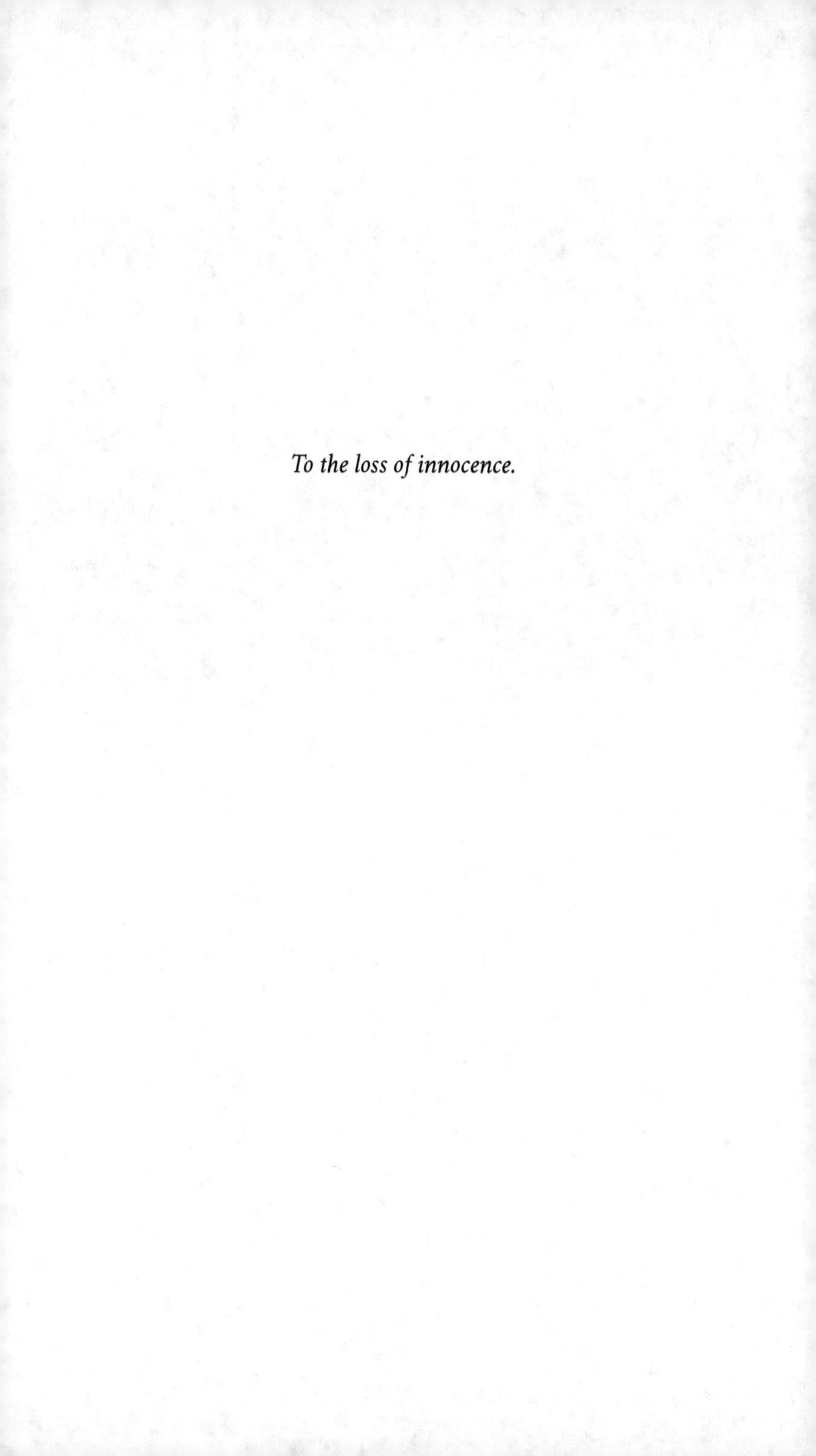

To the loss of innocence.

I

A MECHANICAL EXHALATION AND A RUMBLING SLIDE AS SIXTEEN sets of doors open simultaneously. Foot after foot after foot after foot, stepping out and striding along the uneven concrete and grey, cracked tarmac. Wanton high heels, business brogues, slouchy trainers, sensible court shoes, unseasonal flip-flops. On and on they walk, one after another after another, close enough to touch. Yet all mouths are silent and all heads are bowed.

A grating mechanical voice echoes off the high tin roof, ignored by almost all.

– The oh-nine hundred train to Guildford will depart from platform eleven, calling at Clapham Junction, Surbiton, Woking and Guildford. First class accommodation can be found at the front of the train. Tickets may not be bought on this service.

The column of bowed heads splits as it reaches the top of the platform. Most dart for the Underground, while others search giant boards for onward connections. One head picks its way through the unyielding crowds, pushing for a far-off exit. It's a beautiful day, why not walk? Why not indeed.

Suitcases and crouching children, milling tourists and leafleteers; rubbish carts with stowed brushes, advertising boards, café-style seating and roped-off areas. Eventually he reaches the station exit, his shiny leather shoes clicking down the metal-edged steps. On and on now, across the road and away from the pockmarked imperial excess of Waterloo station, under the rail bridge and on to Royal Festival Hall.

Up the steps, two by two by two, his tie flapping in the spring breeze. The weak sunlight fades and swells as billowing clouds meander across the sky, their shadows melting and hardening on the still-damp paving stones.

Now up to Hungerford Bridge, ignoring the pleading homeless man and the Chinese street sellers. Threading through the crowds, he pushes on, tracing with tired eyes the outline of the office blocks and the roof of Embankment station. No need to go straight to the office; you can waste a little time. Take a detour, why don't you, and take in the plea-sures of Villiers Street. Have a shot of carefree London.

Down the steps of the suspended bridge and through the milling tourists lost in the Tube station ticket hall, ambling like cows in a farm yard. Out the other side, he ignores the Big Issue seller and breathes in the calm of the rising street, recalling a long-lost evening at Gordon's Wine Bar and her laughter in the vaulted shadows.

His pace slows as he tries to forget the cares of the oncoming day, unbuttoning his pinstriped jacket and loos-ening his grip on his briefcase. A cup of coffee. Yes, there it is, his favourite place. It's full and there's a queue, but he has time to spare.

– Next please.

– An espresso and a blueberry muffin, please.

He watches the young woman with pale, translucent skin type his order into the till and turn to shout to the barista. She turns back and stares emptily at him.

– One espresso and a muffin. £3.25, please.

He gazes at her badge. Magda. Polish? She has an accent, but she could be from anywhere in Eastern Europe.

– £3.25 please.

– Oh, yes, sorry.

He fishes in his trouser pocket. Not enough change. He pulls a crisp five pound note out of his wallet. Magda is still and calm while the café whirs and buzzes around her, all shouted orders and coffee machines hissing in the morning air, a rhythmic cacophony of rustling paper bags and clacking tongs searching racks of pastries, jangling coins passing back and forth and till draws clattering open and shut. He watches the hands reaching across the glass divide, and the cursory exchanges in the confined space behind the counter.

Magda places a coffee cup and a small paper bag on the counter, dropping two serviettes inside.

– One espresso and a blueberry muffin.

He smiles weakly and takes the coffee cup and the bag handles, the folds rough in his office hands.

– Next please.

As the man turns away she sees him for the first time, noting his suited, narrow back and his unfit, sloping shoulders, his thinning hair and the grey flecks nestling within. A woman steps forward to fill the space, erasing his existence.

II

THE FACES COME AND GO IN THE CAFÉ, COME AND GO, flowing up to the glass divide and receding like an endless tide. Receding and breaking, receding and breaking. Everybody different, everybody the same. Men, women, families on holiday, children off school, office secretaries with a complicated order, lazy writers with unkempt hair, dust-laden builders feeling out of place. All reduced to the ebb and flow of faces, coffee and food, loose change and paper money.

The tide wanes. The clock on the wall clicks 10:30 and, on cue, the nicotine cravings crawl through Magda's brain. She pushes through the metal-plated door and into the narrow corridor between the half-empty storerooms and untidy back office, picking up her handbag as she passes.

In a quiet, narrow alleyway behind the café, she pulls out a small packet of cigarettes adorned with a Polish health warning, tasting the filter on her tongue as she places the paper cylinder in her mouth. The flame reaches the tip and she listens to the crackle of dried leaves. She draws the smoke steadily into her lungs, luxuriating in the chemical rush that tingles through her.

Once sated, she takes occasional draws from the cigarette while she looks around the stained and dusty alleyway, at the empty boxes pilled up in a corner and the homeless blanket folded neatly in an unused doorway. She glances up at the roofs over her head. Far above, a pigeon regards her with a glass black eye and flies away. A muffled jingle breaks the near-silence. Magda searches for her phone in the bag, picking up the call on the last ring.

– Hello Anna. Thanks for calling me back. Did you get my message?…Great. Yes, I'm out the back, having a…you've got them? Thank you so much. I'll be outside in a minute.

She crushes the half-smoked cigarette beneath a battered ballet pump and walks through the slowly refilling café. Lunchtime is on its way. Only a little peace left to steal before the tide builds once more.

She sees Anna standing awkwardly by the door. A smile and a moment of indecision. Should she kiss her on the cheek? Anna stole her milk and broke her plate, but she went out of her way to bring her keys. Maybe when she leaves.

The keys rattle as they are pulled from Anna's over-stuffed bag.

For the sake of propriety, of meeting again that evening, of the embarrassment over previous arguments, they chat for too long. Enthusiastically but with nothing to say. Neither knows how to end the conversation, so they stumble over saying they are busy and have to go, and fail to embrace. Tonight will be easier, they hope, now the rituals are re-established.

Magda retreats into the café while Anna walks briskly up Villiers Street. She weaves through the crowds, puts head-phones into her ears and listens to the radio. As she turns onto John Adam Street and away from the bustle, the sun pierces the clouds for a moment and illuminates the Georgian townhouses, modern office buildings, pubs.

The heat builds and she adjusts her cardigan.

The road rises towards Adam Street and she tires, regretting her wasted gym membership and expanding waistline, and opens her cardigan. She smiles at someone from her office walking past. What is his name? Where does he work? Accounts. No. IT? No. Brian, that's it. Client services. Always down the pub. Sailing enthusiast. Leering eyes after four pints. Wandering hands after eight. All that and wife and child. Tsk, tsk. Still, it didn't put Jill off at her leaving drinks. She could've sucked his face off. Slut.

As she reaches her office door she pauses. No need to waste a break. And there's still two hours to lunchtime. She notices two men talking on the other side of the road and absent-mindedly pulls a crumpled packet of cigarettes from her bag. The clouds return and she pulls her cardigan around her, spotting a stain. Bloody cappuccino. She licks her finger and tries to wipe it off but fails. She lights her cigarette and, through the rising smoke, regards the two men at leisure. Both are dressed casually, one very tall, with a beard, giant headphones around his neck and a battered satchel, the other with long hair, faded t-shirt and short jeans. They kick at imaginary stones as they talk and hang their heads like puppets, laughing every now and again. They seem so relaxed, so cool, so effortless. What are they talking about? She pulls the forgotten headphones out of her ears. It sounds like they're talking about a party. I wish I knew them. I don't know any cool people.

She looks away at the sound of a van driving fast down the street and then back to the two men. They perform a complicated handshake and there's more laughter. The bearded one walks away towards Adam Street with a lolling gait, looking around as he goes. Dammit. I should have asked them for a light or something. Maybe I could run after him? Don't be stupid, Anna. You haven't washed your hair and you're wearing a coffee-stained cardigan. And you, young lady, are definitely not cool.

As turns the corner and disappears, she sighs, throwing her cigarette into the gutter, her mind turning back to her desk and the endless emails.

III

THE BEARDED ONE WALKS UP ADAM STREET TOWARDS THE
Strand, hardly noticing the delivery vans, the swarms of
tourists unsure of their destination, the streams of office
workers entering and leaving offices. As he reaches the main
road, the relentless noise and metallic stench of the traffic,
held tight in the tunnel of buildings lining the street, crash
over him.

He gazes at the hoarding on the Adelphi Theatre showing
the latest musical and smiles derisively. Glancing from side
to side, he wonders whether to do the right thing and go to
the nearest crossing. Can't be bothered. In a break in the
traffic, between the black cabs, red buses and cars, he holds
down his headphones and sprints across both sets of lanes,
almost colliding with a cycle courier, and slips into the
narrow, piss-stained Lumley Court.

The cacophony of the Strand falls away and the bearded
one is left in near-silence. As he walks slowly up the alleyway, he examines the steep cliffs of greyed bricks and dirty
white bars covering the lower windows of back offices.

He watches a dark cloud cross the narrow strip of watery blue sky between the tops of the buildings. Great place to film a video. The camera angles would be a bit tight, though. Reaching the steps at the end, he takes them two at a time and turns left into Maiden Lane, quickly crossing the empty road and striding through the crowds. Turning right into Bedford Street, he curses under his breath as he negotiates the slow-moving tourists on the narrow pavement.

After contemplating the back of a balding, middle-aged Frenchman's head and fantasising about pushing him out the way, the bearded one steps into the road, side-stepping parked scooters and black cabs and jumping back onto the pavement as he reaches the junction of Garrick Street and King Street. He emerges from the herd and slows down as he walks up Rose Street and into the Lamb and Flag.

– All right Mark?

Dropping his satchel on the floor, the bearded one slides onto a wooden stool next to Mark and smiles.

– Oh, right. Hi mate. Didn't see you come in there. How are you doing?

– Good, thanks, yeah. You?

– Yeah, all right. Bit hassled, actually. You know, having to come into town. It takes ages to get here from Shoreditch. Why did you want to meet here, anyway? Isn't this a bit of a tourist trap? I had enough trouble dealing with them on the way here.

The bearded one smiles.

– Yeah, right. Old Street would definitely've been better but I've got to meet someone after. I'm doing some work for a guy on Floral Street. He wants fliers for a DJ night he's doing in Soho. So, what do you want? Pint?

– Nah, I got totally mashed last night. I'm not drinking until at least tomorrow. I quite fancy a lemonade, actually.

– What? That's not like you.

– Yeah, I know, right? Totally.

The bearded one buys them both a drink and they sip in silence before the bearded one pulls a small portfolio from his bag and opens it out on the bar. They talk animatedly over a series of designs, watched with growing interest by a man leaning against the bar. As soon as there's a lull in the conversation, the man clears his throat and speaks.

– Nice shoes.

Mark turns quickly and sees the man for the first time. He is smartly dressed, with a vintage tweed jacket over a polo top, and a scarf tossed loosely around his neck. Mark's eyes are drawn to his immaculate beard and moustache, worked into two symmetrical twists at the ends. That and his bright-red face and unsteady focus.

– Nice shoes, the moustachioed man repeats, nodding down to the floor.

They both stare at Mark's giant brown basketball shoes in silence and then at the white Adidas trainers worn by the well-dressed man.

– Thanks, Mark says eventually.

– You might think I'm hardly a good judge of footwear, seeing as I'm wearing the sort of white trainers that might kindly be called 'old skool' but actually are coveted by only the worst kind of wide boy.

The younger men laugh.

– However, I am able to say with confidence that yours are a fine pair.

– Thanks mate.

– I hope I'm not disturbing your conversation, gents, but I couldn't help noticing that you two aren't the usual sort we get in this establishment.

The man waves his arm unsteadily around the room.

– Yeah, talking of which, I have to be going, the bearded

one says, pushing the portfolio back into his bag. – I've got that to meet that guy.

– Oh, right, yeah, Mark says uncomfortably. – See you later.

– Good day to you, sir, the man says loudly. – And good luck with whatever adventures life brings you.

After a brief smile, the bearded one walks across the bar and out into the sunshine, pausing before disappearing around the side of the pub. Mark watches him and wonders how he can extract himself from the pub without get trapped in a conversation. Not so easy now he's bailed and bloody left me in the lurch.

– Yes, the moustachioed man continues. – In a drinking hole such as this, we are surrounded mostly by travellers from far-off lands and desk-slaves, as well as the odd drunken bore like me. The man laughs and places his hand carefully on the bar.

– Unfortunately, I've got to go too, mate, so you'll be left with your usual crowd, I'm afraid.

Mark picks up his bag and slides off the stool.

– I can't blame you, young sir. The man leans forward conspiratorially. – Actually, I have to be moving on too. I've have to see a man in Islington who is in desperate need of some company in his lonely quest for filthy lucre. The only customers he gets in his rarefied boutique nowadays are philistines who wouldn't know proper antique furniture if it came up and slapped them across their well-upholstered behinds. So, I'm going to talk nonsense at him to fill the empty hours until we can respectably call time and repair to the nearest hostelry.

The drunken man laughs uproariously into Mark's face. The young man smiles awkwardly, recoiling from the rancid alcohol on the drunk's breath.

– Right. I know what you mean.

Mark slings his bag over his shoulder.

The man stares at nothing for a second before draining his drink and placing a hand on Mark's shoulder.

– My friend, I wish you every success in all your endeavours, and keep wearing the shoes.

IV

The drunken man watches Mark leave.

– Nice bloke, he says to no one.

With a faint air of disgust, he pushes away his glass and stares into nothing, crushing emotion creeping around the edges of his face. He then snaps back into the room, looks around confused, and leaves.

Outside, the man rocks back and forth on his heels as he regards the passing crowds, then ambles unsteadily down Bedford Street. Bloody tourists. Filling up the pavements like hippos. No idea what they're seeing. The glory of London, laid before their eyes. Wasted on people like that.

Why did he turn around? Am I speaking out loud? Am I shouting? I don't know, and I bloody well don't care.

At the bottom of the street, he turns onto the Strand and reaches the bus stop just as the 91 arrives. After trying several pockets, he produces Travelcard he found on the street the day before and flashes it at the driver. He makes his way down the aisle like a mariner on a storm-tossed ship and falls into a seat next to an elderly woman, flashing her a wide grin as he gathers himself. Surreptitiously, he fishes a flask of gin from his jacket pocket and takes a long swig, revelling in the burning sensation pushing its way down his throat.

Soon it will take hold.

A sparkle flashes across his eyes. He smiles at a young mother across the aisle, who turns instantly away. Another dash of gin and he turns his attention to the road. They leave the Strand, head around Aldwych and up Kingsway. Taxis, buses, delivery vans, cyclists and cars, jostling for space and supremacy. Offices, theatres, cafés, restaurants, museums, colleges and churches, one after another after another after another, zipping past the window. And people, everywhere. Milling tourists and brisk suits, lazy trustafarians and dirty builders, foreign students and homeless drunks.

At least I'm not as bad as them. He fishes the flask from his pocket once more, draining the last drops of delicious nectar. You will never be like that, my friend. Not like them. Never.

The bus lurches away from the traffic lights and onto Southampton Row. Pretty Sicilian Avenue. The white stone and red bricks glow like jewels in the weak sunlight breaking through the rolling clouds. Now gone. All is dark and ugly now. Ugly traffic. Ugly hotels. Ugly tourist shops and ugly offices. Ugly, ugly, *everywhere, not a drop to drink. The very deep did rot: O Christ! That ever this should be! Yea, slimy things did crawl with legs upon the slimy sea*...too much swaying on this bus, feeling sick, rocking bus. Not good...stop swaying...hold the bar, *hold fast that which is good*...

Who is that strange face? I know him, don't I? Turn around so I can see your face better...Don't ask, don't draw attention to yourself...but you could turn round...funny, wheres that petrol station gone? It was there before...oh. No, it isn't him. It's someone else...stop swaying, bus, I need to relieve myself and you're breaking my concentration. Mummy needs relief...Euston or Kings Cross? Concrete ugly or yellow brick ugly? *Follow the yellow brick road / Follow the yellow brick road / Follow, follow, follow, follow...We're off to see the pissard / The wonderful pissard of poz / We hear he is a piss of a piz*...what you staring at? Never seen a man drunk before? It's all part of the wonderful education of living in this great city. I am here to remind you how good you are, you know. To make you realise that your life is better than you think...there's really no need to be afraid...ah, Euston, concrete saviour, the yellow brick road can wait. Shall I stumble into thee, cast my coins at thy feet, pray for bladder salvation, or shall I just express my gratitude on your dusty concrete steps? Better not, mister policeman is looking bored, don't want to give him a chance to extend his long arm...bloody steps, that hurt. no I'm fine, thank you never better...shoddy workmanship, typical of this once-great city, collapsing to its knees. and shall I take a train, shall I leave and be rocked into slumber on the whatever to wherever?

ah the pissard of poz. better see him first. coins perhaps, or maybe I shall just sneak in behind this accommodating chap in the suit. smartly dressed but dandruff. no need to look so offended, I don't want to bugger you…ah, that feels better I could put out a fire with that...what did he say? *I voided in such a quantity and applied so well to the proper places that in three minutes the fire was wholly extinguished and the rest of that noble pile which had cost so many ages in erecting preserved from destruction*...funny bugger. I suppose I'd better leave. bloody attendant watching me suspicious, of what, I don't know. what? does he think I'm going to steal his mop or some paper towels? not much of a black market for those. oh, my hands, not working so well. can't seem to...

blurred lights, incomprehensible noise, faces close by,

coin on the floor, can't bend or would fall, feet, feet, feet, shiny floor, upside down suitcase. bang. elbow hurt, don't help me up, then, you...your face looks like...yes, could be yellow, red-blue neon, endless corridor, tunnel and darkness. can't seem to find my way. how am I ever going to...get a hold of yourself, just go the right way to...open space, hundreds of people, wide light, floor shining, shiny. growling announcement, clicking feet, rolling wheels, food, staring people, staring policeman, policewoman, whatever... hat hair tied back, hair girl with large teddy...record store, could steal some...no, can't lift my hands...anyway, they would see and I can't run on this floor. bad feet, my bad feet. where is exit leave? want outside fresh air, feel trapped in shiny floor and clicking heels, want to see green, not yellow, red-blue neon, automatic door. confusing, went to push but almost fell over. don't laugh, bloody student, with nothing to do, lazy bugger, never done a day's...that's better, fresh air at last

HOW DID I cross the street? car going past fast, making sick feeling rise in stomach, can't be right. straight feet, all over the place. BE STRAIGHT. WALK PROPERLY. can't, lost all bearings. no, not bearings, something else. maybe have a rest. where is this? no, don't stand here next to the bloody transformation shop. people will think I want to become a woman. fake tits and a shaved chest. bit further, lean on that tree, *Lean on me, when you're not strong,* keep going for tree. no, you're veering again, you bugger, weaving like a woven carpet. mother's woven carpet...looked Arabic but it was a fake surel,...no, feet. GO THE OTHER WAY. you're a bit hard, young tree, hope it doesn't rattle your leaves to bump into you like that...brown...concrete...tarmac...paving stones...feet, bloody feet. hell...what's that? a taxi, a black bulbous shadow? that woman in the back, her black eyes catching me in her black widow's web, spun to…I see you. yes, you, black widow woman, I'm looking at you…off you go, off you go to Camden, you black, black shadow. godspeed and god riddance…

V

THE BLACK SHADOW CRAWLS UP EVERSHOLT STREET, PAST THE concrete cliff of Euston station and the jumble of newsagents, pubs, casinos and adult shops cowering in its shade; past the tired blocks of flats, worn-out convenience stores, toothless grand Victorian terraces; and past the polluted and stained trees, tenaciously clinging to life.

As the taxi slides past Mornington Crescent tube station and climbs Camden High Street, the woman, sitting deep in the back, looks up from her files and open laptop and gazes out of the window. Drug addicts, drunks and the homeless, dragging their possessions, arguing, stumbling, all flaying their souls for a sip of tepid beer on the dirty pavement. She shudders.

And then they are gone.

The cab turns left up Delancey Street. Modest terraces and nestling pubs drift past the windows. The woman sighs and looks back down at her files. It's nearly done. There's not much point in doing any more at this point. She shuffles the files back into order and closes her computer, then inspects her fingernails. Bloody nail varnish. It's already chipped.

That was new on yesterday. What a rip-off. She lifts her hands into the light. But they're not so bad. They don't look old, do they. My skin's still okay, not too many lines. They certainly don't look like a fifty-year-old's hands. A decade younger, even.

She folds her hands on her lap. I wonder if he'll be there? She thinks about checking her face in her mirror. How long has it been? Three weeks? I really shouldn't have got so drunk with him before he went on holiday. And I most definitely should have stayed in the pub with the others. What the hell were you thinking? Maybe he'll blank you. Would that be worse than him being rude or, horror of horrors, trying to explain himself?

She looks out of the window again. The cab is crossing Parkway and gliding along Oval Road. Aren't they beautiful houses? Didn't I see Alan Bennett down there once? He looked old. But then he is old. She gazes down towards Gloucester Crescent. A flat there must cost a bomb. Mind you, I couldn't bear waking up next to all that Camden Market madness on a Saturday morning.

Her stomach tightens as a stained white stuccoed office block looms into view and the cab slowly draws to a halt.

– That'll be twelve ninety-five.

She pulls fifteen pounds out of her purse and pushes it through the small window and into the waiting hand.

– Keep the change.

– Thanks, love.

– Can I have a receipt?

She opens the door and awkwardly pulls out her bag and laptop. She waits by the driver's window, straightening her dark blue business suit and checking the top button of her blouse.

– Here you go, love. Have a good day.

– And you.

Neither smiles. Neither cares.

The cab swings away from her and she takes the steps up to the glass doors of the stained stuccoed building, pushing them open with a shove. The reception is empty and the grey walls, adorned with cheap reprints of Kandinsky and Klee, seem forlorn and hopeless.

– Lovely, she says to no one.

Two young men talk noisily as they climb the stairs from the basement office.

– Yeah, it was a massive night, one says, carefully gauging the other's reaction. – I was totally wasted. I had, like, ten pints. Then, at closing time, Mark dragged me off clubbing. It was rubbish. You know, that place we always go? I seriously don't know why we bother. Still, two, like, well-fit girls who had been eyeing me up for hours gave me their number. I even nearly snogged one of them. I've only had about two hours sleep, it was mental.

The other young man smiles. He thinks of his quiet night at home watching a nature programme.

– Yeah, sounds totally mental, he says. I mean, I had, like, just a few pints with some mates, but I'm totally saving myself for the weekend. Got a mental party coming up. Oh, hi Natalie. You're late today.

– Yes. The woman stares at the two men. – I had to go to an eight am meeting with potential clients in the West End.

Their eyes glaze over.

– Oh, right. Sounds, like, high level. Any more business?

– Some, maybe. But the negotiations are always slow.

– Right, totally, they say emptily.

– Anyway, I must have to report to David. You two are out for an early lunch. She looks at her watch. 12:15.

– Yeah, right. Feeding a hangover. Know what I mean?

The two men laugh and push through the glass doors.

The woman watches their backs as they disappear from view.

– Losers.

The two men cross Oval Road and descend the steps to Regent's Canal towpath.

– Where shall we go? That pub up Chalk Farm Road does a, like, well-good all-day breakfast.

– Ace. I want to go through Camden Market anyway. I was thinking of getting a t-shirt I saw last week with a big cannabis leaf on it and the words 'Stoner for Life' written underneath.

They both laugh.

– Wow, that's totally mental. You should wear it to work.

They both laugh again.

By the time they climbed the humped bridge, they are in silence. A gaggle of teenagers lounge at the summit, staring at everyone who passes. The smell of weed hangs thick in the air, and the two men breathe deeply. As they descend towards the market, they look at each other and smile.

– We could just stand around and get, like, totally stoned for free.

– Yeah, right. Totally.

They turn into the market and plunge into the maelstrom. Sizzling spicy vegetable stir fries; racks of T-shirts swaying on breeze-blown hangars; soul music blaring out of battered speakers; cheap jewellery glistening in the sunshine; dark wooden African art; sickly sweet ice cream, slowly melting; piles of tired German army coats; packs of tarot cards displayed on tie-dyed cloth; vintage jackets and skirts; shabby Eastern trinkets; piles of seventies glassware; wicker furniture spilling out onto the walkways. And shoulders, arms, backs; pushing, jostling, barging, all close enough to smell. Sallow faces, blond dreadlocks, straggly beards, sharp eyes, stained teeth; old drunks, young punks, stoners, hippies, dropouts, all seeking a way out of something they cannot define.

The two men push through the crowds and down the steps.

– I think the place is along here somewhere.

They turn right and then left, following the maze of paths between rows and rows of clothes and trinket stalls. They stop and stare at a woman dressed in a loose kaftan and headscarf, busying herself at a jewellery stall. She is small and blonde, with a pixie face and an indefinable beauty and grace.

– Okay, see you later. She gives a key to a much taller and larger woman standing behind the stall and smiles. – I'll be back in about an hour. Thanks for looking after it.

– No problem, babes, the taller woman says.

The young blonde woman looks up and notices the two men. I wonder what they're staring at. Losers.

VI

The young woman pushes out from behind her stall and onto the walkway. She strides, her kaftan flowing, and glances around as she goes, absorbing the blur of colours, sounds and smells. At her favourite stall, she buys a box of mixed-vegetable stir fry and threads between the shops and stalls, past the displays of fetish gear and goth clothes and through the fast-growing lunchtime crowd. Eventually, she reaches the gate and turns left onto Chalk Farm Road, flinching at the metallic stench of fumes from the roaring buses and the endless stream of cars and taxis. Passing the petrol station and supermarket, she wonders, as she does every day, how something so bland and faceless could have been built there. But she soon forgets it as she sees the Roundhouse, the last vestige of quirky, shabby, charming Camden before it melts into Chalk Farm. She glances at her watch. 12:45. Not much time left. Better hurry. She darts into Regent Park Road and across the bridge over the railway tracks. And on, past rows and rows of terraces dotted with pubs, blending into tiny shops, off-licences and cafés, as the rich green of Primrose Hill slides into view.

She sprints across the road, narrowly avoiding the passing cars, and on through the gate into the park, slowing as she begins to climb. Clouds fill the sky; rolling, billowing masses of white-grey, blocking out all traces of blue. A cold breeze blows across the side of the hill and she shivers. Walking up the tarmac path, she watches excited dogs chasing bouncing balls and ambling tourists with backpacks discussing…she has no idea what. A drunk she recognises pulls a filthy duvet around his shoulders, screwing his eyes up against the wind, and two plastic kites circle in the air, their owners calling to each other animatedly. All the while, the grass, uncut for weeks, ripples and flows in the wind.

The summit is in sight and her legs being to tire. Too much booze. I've got to cut down. And all those cigarettes. How many last night? At least a packet. She feels in her pocket. Are there some left? At least one. I can't really afford any more. I haven't sold nearly enough jewellery this week. God, how am I going to make it to the end of the month? I still haven't paid the rent, and I'm supposed to be going out for John's birthday drinks tonight. Maybe I can borrow some money, or not drink anything. No, not drinking would make it worse, and I'd just feel pathetic and helpless.

As she reaches the top of the hill, she pauses, seeing if there is space on the benches away from everyone. Nothing suitable. She turns and London spreads itself before her, the hill falling away to reveal a patchwork of grey-brown behind the treetops. Centre Point and the BT Tower rise up towards the overcast sky, outstretched arms appealing to the heavens.

She tries to remember what it feels like to be excited by the view, to be excited by being above the city, by seeing all that life, potential, danger laid out at her feet. But she feels nothing. She doesn't even try to pick out her flat as she does normally.

A crow circles, and pigeons peck at the crumbs near her

feet. She looks at the box of vegetable stir fry, the sauce congealing in the cold breeze, and considers throwing it away. No, I can't do that. It wouldn't be right.

She finds an empty patch of grass and sits. The cold of the ground pushes through her kaftan. For the first time in months, she feels lonely, empty, lost. She stabs disconsolately at the stir fry, unwilling to eat even one mouthful. John's birthday. Maybe I could just miss it, just not turn up. I could turn off my mobile and have a bath.

But aren't I supposed to be in love? Aren't I supposed to care? But maybe he wouldn't even notice if I didn't turn up. We hardly see each other nowadays. And he only ever seems happy when he's surrounded by his mates, talking about music and the band. Perhaps no one would notice if I wasn't there. Wouldn't it be nice just to slip away and disappear, to be forgotten instantly?

What about that guy, the one in the bar last week? He seemed so…oh, shut up. He seemed great because he wasn't John. He kissed nicely, though, didn't he? Soft, slow. He seemed a bit needy, but then the sensitive types always are.

She puts down the stir fry and pulls at the blades of grass by her leg, sighing to herself. A drop of rain hits her arm and she shivers again, waking her from her thoughts. What's the time? 13:15. Damn. Damn. Mary'll be wanting to get back to her stall.

Squashing the lid back onto the stir fry, she runs down the hill, watching the heavy, full drops of rain paint black polka dots on the tarmac path. The drunk is gone and the dogs are following their owners home. The tourists scurry to shelter and the wind blows hard, forcing the grass into waves.

As she runs on and on, her lungs burst, and she realises she will never make it if she keeps up this pace. But the rain and wind on her face makes her feel alive. Just.

At the bottom of the hill, she rounds the gate and runs straight into a tall man in a raincoat. The box of stir fry flies out of her hand and lands hard, bursting open, scattering yellow vegetables and noodles and congealed sauce across the pavement. She starts to cry, small at first, then sobbing, her tears mingling with the rain.

– Are you okay? I'm so sorry. I didn't…

– It doesn't matter, she mutters. – It doesn't matter.

She turns and runs away, on and on, between the traffic and back along Regent's Park Road. The tall man in the raincoat watches her until he can see her no more.

VII

THE MAN TURNS AWAY, WORRIED ABOUT THE BEAUTIFUL woman with pixie face. The rain is teeming now and he bows his head, tucking his chin into the folds of his raincoat. His hair is wet, and the water runs in rivulets down his collar.

I should've done more to help her, I should've stopped her running away and talked to her. But she was so determined.

He looks back to where she ran, half expecting her to appear around the corner. But there is no one, just a couple of tourists with the hoods of their plastic jackets pulled down over their foreheads. He purses his lips and blows drops of water from his mouth. It's too late to think about her now.

He walks slowly, absentmindedly along Regent's Park Road, narrowly avoiding tripping over a grey electricity box. Remembering that he has a destination and a time to meet, he begins to stride, causing the rain to run down the back of his neck. I'm going to be late. Andy won't be happy.

On he walks, following the edge of the park, turning onto Primrose Hill Road. The park is soon left behind, replaced by rows of houses and streets to cross. But none of it reaches him. The girl with the pixie face and his meeting with Andy crowd his mind.

At Adelaide Road, he almost steps into the line of traffic, just checking himself in time. He squints into the rain and watches the cars and vans stream past, water flying up from their tyres. Puddles are forming, and he has to step back from the pavement edge as a bus rolls by and sends an arc of water through the metal posts of the barrier and onto the sodden slabs, narrowly missing his feet.

The lights change and he steps onto the crossing ahead of the small crowd gathered behind him. What time is it? I don't want to check my mobile, It'll get wet. He flicks the collar of his raincoat up around his neck. He imagines himself in a sixties spy drama and almost laughs out loud at his pretension.

At England's Lane, he turns right and looks up before he crosses the road, spotting a middle-aged woman staring from a first-floor window. She stands, hands on hips, apparently seeing nothing. The man darts between the parked cars and onto the other pavement, wondering what the woman is thinking about.

He forgets her as he turns left onto Haverstock Hill, passing lines of shops before striding up to a half-hidden door and pressing the top bell.

– Hello. Hi Andy. Yep, it's me.

– Great, come up, the metallic voice crackles back.

The door buzzes and clicks, and the man pushes it open. He pauses on the woven mat to shake out his coat and run a hand over his hair. I must look a state.

He trudges slowly up the carpeted stairs, passing closed doors shrouded in half-light. At the top, he knocks gently on the door, which opens almost immediately.

– Oh my God, look at you. You're soaked.

– Yes, it's tipping it down out there.

– I didn't realise. I've been messing around in the kitchen for ages. Let's get you out of that coat.

Andy takes the tall man's raincoat and disappears into the bathroom, reappearing with a towel, which he thrusts into his hand.

– It's for your hair.

– Thanks.

Andy stops as he passes into the living room.

– Oh, I didn't say hello. He turns and smiles at the tall man. – Hello Stephen.

– Hello Andy.

The two men kiss briefly on the lips and hug.

– Come in, lunch is nearly ready.

– Great, thanks. Sorry I'm late.

– Not at all. I'd only just put the pasta on.

Andy disappears into the kitchen as Stephen saunters around the living room, noticing for the first time the soft dance music playing from the stereo. He glances at the covers of the magazines arranged tastefully on the coffee table, making a mental note of a couple he would like to read. Then he looks in the mirror above the obsolete fireplace and laughs at his reflection.

– I look terrible, he calls out.

– No, hun, just wet.

Stephen smiles to himself and walks over to the bookcase. On the second shelf down, between a Martin Amis novel and an anthology of Auden, stands a theremin.

– This is new, Stephen shouts to the kitchen.

The clattering of pots and pans from the kitchen stops.

– Oh, you mean the theremin?

– Yes, when did you get that?

– Last week I think. I was pottering about in a lovely little shop in Hampstead. I thought we could use it for the recording.

Stephen fingers the metal antenna.

– Yes, maybe we could. I hadn't thought of using something like that. Actually, on that subject, I've had a few ideas for our next studio session.

The sound of water running into a metal saucepan drifts in from the kitchen.

– Great, we can talk about them over lunch. Also, this CD I'm playing might be useful. It's by that guy you met at Anthony's party last week.

– Right. I remember, Stephen lies. – Nice guy.

– He was indeed.

Stephen walks over to the window and gazes down on Haverstock Hill. Pensioners in clear plastic hoods with cheap, market-stall coats pass by. A girl runs through the rain in a summer dress. An estate agent strides by with a newspaper over his head. Two old men chatting under an awning, with a collie standing guard. Three buses, shining in the endless rain, rolling by, then a black cab, and cars, cars, cars. Trees swaying in the breeze and a pigeon coming into land next to a dropped burger. And what about the girl with the pixie face? Where is she?

Stephen turns from the window and calls out.

– You know, I bumped into a girl today. Literally. I was on my way here. I knocked her lunch clean out of her hand and it went all over the pavement.

The clattering of plates from the kitchen stops.

– You should have bought her another lunch.

– I would've done, but she started crying and ran away before I could even think. It looked like it must've been the final straw for her, like it tipped her over the edge. I'm a bit worried, to be honest. Maybe something terrible has happened to her and…I don't know…maybe she's going to do something stupid.

The plates stop clattering.

– But how would you find her?

– I don't know. Stephen pauses. – That's the problem.

A ladle is tapped several times on a plate.

– Well, I'm sure she'll sort herself out. It's sad, but there isn't much you can do, hun.

Stephen turns back to the window. – No, he says softly to himself. – I wish there was, though.

A couple walking out of a nearby house catches his eye. They are laughing and look up to the heavens, obviously complaining light-heartedly about the rain. The girl, with short hair and dressed in a flowing top and slim jeans, is lithe and pretty, just like the boy, whose slacker-chic clothes compliment hers.

The perfect couple, Stephen thinks to himself as the boy grabs the girl's hand and pulls her over to a vintage VW Beetle. The boy unlocks the nearside door and she dives in while he runs around to the other side, watching the traffic before pulling open his own door and jumping in. After a few seconds, the car shudders into life and pulls out into the stream of traffic. Stephen turns away as he hears Andy's footsteps.

– Lunch is served.

VIII

AT FIRST, THE GIRL AND BOY DON'T SAY ANYTHING, ONCE THEIR breathless laughter had subsided in the still of the car. He concentrates on driving and she looks out of her window, biting her fingernails as she stares emptily at people running from the rain. She pulls one one foot out of its shoe and places it on the dashboard.

Whining and shivering, the car slowly rolls up Haverstock Hill towards a line of waiting traffic. The windows steam up from the sudden warmth of their breath in the stale air. Outside, the glass teems with raindrops, driven hard onto the surface, merging and splitting under the force of the wind. The windscreen wipers, slow and ungainly, creak and leave stains as they pass.

– Could you, like, wipe the windows for me? I can't see a thing.

He glances at the girl, who says nothing but unhooks her foot and reaches for a cloth lying in the dirty footwell. She rubs the glass, knocking the rear view mirror out of place. He glances at her again and readjusts the mirror. She stares at the traffic.

– It's going to take, like, a total age. I thought you said it would be, like, quicker at lunchtime.

– I guess everyone else had the same idea.

She leans forward and pushes a cassette into the stereo. A pop anthem blasts out of the speakers and they both start singing.

Once the traffic gets moving, the car crawls past rain-soaked trees, blocks of flats, set-back houses, parked cars and bus stops, and then shops, awnings, pubs, telephone boxes, Tube stations, and people, people, people. But everything is greyed, refracted, blended in the rain-stained glass. They pass a hospital and the tarmac melts into Rosslyn Hill, then flows up to boutiques, bookshops, cafés, and the studied carelessness of Hampstead High Street.

They notice the Hampstead crêpe stall as they pass, even now with a small queue huddled against the rain under the tiny awning, and exchange glances. She laughs.

– Having, like, a crêpe? In this weather? That's totally mad.

He laughs.

– Yeah, totally.

He stops behind a taxi near the top of the hill and watches a woman in her mid-fifties, dressed in a Barbour jacket and Hunter wellies, striding between the cars, pulling two giant, shaggy Labradors behind her, her grey hair matted with rain. He imagines the woman walking through the lanes and back streets of Hampstead, past the piled-up, overblown Victorian redbrick houses, the black-painted rails, the cobbles and the old cars. He thinks of her reaching the Heath and striding through the long grass, feeling the soft earth beneath her wellies, then pulling a dirty, tooth-marked tennis ball from her pocket and throwing it, the dogs splashing through puddles as the run after it. He smiles.

– I want a dog. It would be totally brilliant.

The girl stares at him.

– The flat is, like, no way big enough.

– Yeah, I know. But one day. I definitely want one.

The car, set free from the traffic caravan, sprints unsteadily up and along Heath Street, then slows again in the shadow of the trees along North End Way. Now past the rail depot, past the station and along Golders Green Road. Smaller shops, smaller houses, smaller horizons. And flats ungainly piled.

Under a railway bridge, a moment or two spent dawdling behind a bus, then past a million estate agents, endless blocks and houses, and on and on, towards the stained and sooted bracelet laid around London: the vibrating, restless North Circular.

Singing along to a different pop tune, the girl and boy turn left to join the perpetual migration past Brent Cross, past endless brick, glass and concrete shielding giant shops and faceless offices, past the blue line to The North, past the Welsh Harp and its tilting, dipping sails, past metal ribbons woven through fume-greyed houses, past gardens, roads, past Neasden.

Then they slip away. Away from the noisy tarmac, the shuddering air. They slip around and underneath it, along high blank walls, between warehouses and vast superstores. Then finally, gratefully, contentedly gliding to a halt outside the unbeatable value, the unbearable ubiquity, the unbreakable conformity of the blue-and-yellow Scandinavian middle-class Mecca.

The rain has stopped. The girl and boy slam their doors shut and walk hand-in-hand, their pace quickening as they near their longed-for shopping experience, their chance to cast their love in moulded plastic, veneered chipboard and dyed fabrics. They smile at another older, more well-off couple pushing cardboard boxes into the back of a 4x4. The couple do not smile back and the girl and boy pass, but wordlessly slam the boot, push away their trolley, get in and drive away.

IX

THE SILENCE WEIGHS HEAVY IN THE 4X4, PRESSING IN FROM the windows and doors as they join the slow procession of cars inching their way around London. The woman, in a white shirt with the collar up far enough to meet the hardened curls of her coiffured hair, stares out of the window, wishing she could run somewhere, anywhere. The man glances at her from time to time, flexing his hands on the steering wheel and cursing every hesitation by the cars in front.

– Could you just watch your temper when you drive?

– It's those bloody idiots. They don't know what they're doing. We'll end up having an accident at this rate.

– We'll definitely have an accident if you keep being so angry.

– What? What do you mean? Are you saying there's something wrong with my driving? I'll have you know...

– Don't start, for God's sake Corrine. I just mean you're more likely to hit someone if you're distracted.

– How dare...

– Chris, look at the road!

She instinctively thrusts her hand onto the leather dashboard, bracing herself as the 4x4 swerves and almost mounts the pavement to avoid a pizza delivery driver on a moped. They say nothing as they rejoin the line of traffic and catch their breath.

– Damn fool didn't look where he was going.

– It's always someone else's fault, isn't it. When are you going to accept you aren't perfect?

– I don't know what you're talking about.

They lapse into silence and Corrine stares out of the window again, alone in the 4x4 with an unknown man she calls her husband.

The drift along the North Circular, hemmed in by rails, then red and yellow brick walls covered with graffiti, the distances marked off by lampposts, lampposts, lampposts, beating time to their silent journey. They pass a tower block that looks like…what? A cheese grater?

They pass beneath roads, electric trains, footbridges, all heavy grey against the heavy grey sky, rolling on and on in the company of articulated lorries, dirty transit vans and cement mixers, parcel vans, cars and buses. The green verges lie cluttered with plastic wrappers, drinks cartons, cigarette packets and empty water bottles thrown from passing windows without a passing thought, gathered by the winds into an exhibition of carelessness.

A red-and-grey warehouse breaks up the brown-and-grey monotony under the grey skies. The clouds part for an instant and a burst of light catches on the dirty glass of an anonymous stopover hotel.

They slow down and Corrine glimpses into 1930s flats and empty office blocks. Car showrooms and adverts for TV shows they will never watch glide past the window; a giant Chinese restaurant and self-storage; diggers poised on flatbed trucks; folded cranes on their way to lift the city into the sky; mock Tudor dwellings opening straight onto the traffic torrent; a lighting wholesaler.

The trees return and she watches their graceful sway in the rising wind, incongruous in the wasteland corridor. A line of shops flashes by and they slow for a giant roundabout and the roads not taken.

As they twist towards the south, the world twists a quarter turn, transforming into parks, smart flats and the neighbourhood watch. She thinks to warn him to watch his speed, but she imagines his snapped response and carries on staring out the window, smiling to herself at the thought of him being fined.

The road is clear now and they roll on through the calm of the leafy green. Jaguars jostle with BMWs and Mercs, all wary of the white vans and rumbling lorries. Ealing Common passes by unnoticed in their tree-lined tarmac tunnel.

– Why on earth did you make us go to IKEA today, of all days?

– What? Corrine snaps out of her reverie and stares at him, almost surprised to see him next to her. – What did you say?

– Why did we have to make that stupid journey, just to buy some bloody candles and that stuff for the dining room? We could've done that any time.

– But your friends from the golf club are coming over tonight. I wanted to make the place look nice.

– It looks nice already.

– You know what I mean.

– No. I don't.

– Look, Chris, you saw their place when we went round there last week. It's all tasteful and chic and modern. Ours looks so old and frumpy. I don't want them thinking we're not up-to-date.

– Christ, who cares what they think?

– You do.

– What do you mean?

– You care a lot about what they think.

– No I don't.

– Come off it. You told me in the car on the way home not to screw up this dinner. We've got to impress them, you said.

– I don't remember saying that.

– Well, you did. And you do care, about what everyone thinks of you. I've never met anyone as vain as you.

– What are you talking about? You're talking rubbish again.

– Oh yes? Am I? Just take a look at yourself in the mirror. Look at your hair, for Christ's sake, all gelled up like a teenager to hide your bald patch. And that bloody perma-tan. Who are you trying to kid? Everyone can see how old you really are.

Chris grips the steering wheel and clenches his jaw.

– Oh yes, and you're not vain, Ms bloody dyed-hair-and-too-much-makeup? No amount of slap is going to hide your crow's feet and drink problem, you know.

Corrine purses her lips to stop herself from retaliating. She wants to scratch his eyes out, but she just folds her arms and shoves herself further into her seat.

She stares out of the window as they cross Kew Bridge. The brown torrent of the Thames rages underneath them, but she doesn't see it. She is holding back the tears and wondering whether tonight will be the night she finally plucks up the courage to leave him.

The 4x4 turns off the main road and trundles along the back streets until they pull to a stop outside their white painted semi, a house that, anywhere else, would be ordinary.

She watches him get out of the car and slam the door shut, and wonders where it all went wrong.

Did it ever go right?

If I leave him, where will I go, how will I live? Is it better to stumble on through life unhappy but have everything you want, or be happy but have to start all over again with nothing? She imagines taking a dirty flat in a dirty part of town, full of people from God knows where and shudders. I'd lose everything, everyone. What would it do to our son?

She watches him in the rear-view mirror as he pushes his designer sunglasses up his forehead and grabs at the IKEA boxes in the boot. The bare patches of his scalp show through the gaps in his gelled hair and she thinks of his hairy paunch, sweaty in the sun on their friend's yacht last summer.

She looks down at her own body, a little tired but still in good shape for her age, and she wonders if she could cope with rejection from someone better looking than her husband. At least he will never abandon me, that's for sure.

She pushes open her door as he is walking by, his arms laden with boxes.

– Put the kettle on, will you, Chris calls over his shoulder. – I'll start unpacking these.

Corrine gets out and sees a middle-aged gay couple chatting happily as they wander along the pavement on the other side of the road. A pang of jealousy tugs at her to see their shared comfort and she sighs as she pushes the car door shut.

– Better the devil you know, she says to no one.

X

The two men amble around the back streets of Kew, crossing the railway line and following the road round to Kew Gardens station.

– I always think it looks like a little house, don't you, the taller one asks as the low, yellow brick building comes into view.

– Hmm. Bet it'd cost a fortune to buy it, though. And then you'd still have to renovate it. Can you imagine the parties, though? It'd be fabulous.

– Oh yes, I can see it now. And our guests could just fall into the Tube when they're ready to go home.

– But how would we stop the public coming through our house?

– We'd give them that bit on the side, the bit that that looks like a shed.

– Oh yes. How very kind.

They reach the entrance and pass straight through the ticket office, grateful to have only two minutes to wait on the exposed platform for the next train to central London. The men look up at the clouds, now a lowering mass of metal. Moisture hangs heavy in the air.

– Did you bring an umbrella? The taller one watches an old woman rearranging her shopping bags on the opposite platform, wondering if she will get soaked before she gets home.

– Oh, no, I didn't. You don't think it'll rain again, do you?

– My dear, it's a question of 'when', not 'if'.

The smaller of the two looks up to the sky and pulls his scarf a little closer around his neck.

– Maybe we'll be lucky.

– *Now the world's our lucky highway / All the signs are going my way…*

– What's that from?

– *With a lucky star to guide me / And the one I love beside me…* It's Lucky Me. You know, the Doris Day musical?

– Gosh, I haven't seen that since…actually, I don't think I've seen it all.

– It's wonderful. Well, it has Doris in it, so it is, by definition, wonderful.

The smaller one goes to reply but the train trundles into the station and they ready themselves, trying to spot any free seats as it slows to a stop.

Once inside, they make themselves comfortable and take in the smattering of passengers. No one catches their interest and they lapse into silence, awaiting the off.

Eventually, the doors rumble shut and the train jerks into action, pulling them along the District Line, a green highway from the reassuring tranquillity of Kew to the grinding mill of London proper. Station after station, their names wreathed in forgotten histories: Gunnersbury, Turnham Green, Stamford Brook and Ravenscourt Park; Hammersmith, Barons Court, West Kensington and the seedy glamour of Earl's Court; each offering an exchange of passengers, their dress and style hinting at the streets above. The two men chatter, gossip and comment on the other passengers, their words lost in the screeching rattle of the Tube.

Finally the train enters the inner circle, the cashmere embrace of rich, rich London. At South Ken, the two men alight into the echoing, brightly lit corridors and take the Piccadilly line east, sweeping them under the V&A, Harrods and Harvey Nicks; under the French Embassy, the Iron Duke's square and the Hard Rock Cafe, the Athenaeum, the Ritz and the Wolseley; Burlington Arcade, the Royal Academy and Fortnum & Mason; then under the neon-lit, rubbish-strewn, traffic-choked island of Piccadilly Circus, poisoning the tourist dream with fast food and sleepless commerce.

As the Corporate Blue train slides into the dated pink of Leicester Square station, the two men ready themselves, straightening their clothes after their epic Journey from the West. They smile briefly at each other before the doors open and then push through the mass of dazed tourists waiting on the other platform and up the stairs to the escalators.

– Ooh, there it is, the smaller man says as they take up their positions one step apart on the rising staircase.

– What?

– The play.

The taller one turns and stares through the crowd on the opposite escalator to the row of posters.

– Oh yes, so it is. I read they hadn't sold out. Not even close. I wonder how long it'll last.

– Hmm. I suppose we wouldn't be going if Olivia hadn't done the lighting.

– Quite right, dear. The reviews were awful, poor things.

They lapse into silence again, just two among the hundreds of statues slowly rising towards the ticket hall.

They make their way through the melée rushing by in all directions and head to their exit. At the top of the steps, they and several others tarry in the shelter of the doorway, watching the rain cascade down.

– I told you we should've brought that umbrella.

– Yes, I'm sorry. It completely slipped my mind.

They gaze at the darkening sky and the thick, heavy drops beating down on the shining black pavement.

– At least we don't have far to go.

– Yes, we shouldn't get too wet.

– And we can order a lovely glass of sherry when we get there.

– Ooh, yes. Shall we?

They hesitate for a moment and the smaller of the two glances out at the crowd. He sees a young man in his mid-twenties striding down Charing Cross Road towards Trafalgar Square, purposeful but vulnerable, then disappear into the crowd.

XI

THE YOUNG MAN MARCHES ON DOWN CHARING CROSS ROAD, trying to ignore the rain running down his forehead and the back of his neck. His hair is plastered to his head, and he can sense the encroachment of the cold and damp into his clothes. His shoes have a split somewhere towards the toes, and his jacket is thin and inadequate against the weather. He thinks about his other, more appropriate clothes at home and his umbrella, and curses himself for not checking the forecast before he left.

You always do this, don't you, he mumbles to himself, his lips wet and dripping water as they move. You never prepare. What were you doing on your day off, for Christ's sake? Maybe you want things to go wrong. Maybe that's what you secretly desire.

He looks around. The pavements are full with bowed heads and jostling umbrellas, oblivious in their rush to get out of the rain, and the road roars with cabs and buses, splashing through the growing puddles.

As the road twists around the National Portrait Gallery, the young man pauses. The rain is slowing, and a thin, golden light reaches over the pitched gallery roof. It's quicker to cut through by St Martins and then down to Charing Cross Station, but I want to see the light over Trafalgar Square. He pulls his old and scratched phone out of his sodden jeans and checks the time. I'd only be a a few minutes late, and I don't want to miss something beautiful.

He pockets the phone and trudges on towards the light. The rain softens and the passing crowds lift their heads and slow their step. As he rounds the National Gallery and arrives at Trafalgar Square, the rain lessens to a fine mist, refracting the evening light, filling the sky with a soft golden glow.

The young man stands at the edge of the square, mesmerised by the shimmering light and the reflections on the glistening pavements. People pass and the buses and taxis glide by, but he sees nothing save the golden glow.

He spots a man in a kilt and white t-shirt in front of the steps down to the fountains, playing the bagpipes to no one and everyone. The sound barely pierces the soft rain enough to reach the young man in his far corner, but the tears well as he hears the strains of Flower of Scotland. He thinks of the family he never knew north of the border, the smell of his grandmother's greasy cooking and the stories of his uncle's funeral. He remembers his grandfather's thick Glaswegian accent and his silent canary, and how it started singing the day after he died.

The young man turns away, not wanting to see the piper stop and pack away his things, and starts for Duncannon Street. At the traffic lights, he pauses. The cold of his wet clothes seeps into his skin. A soft muskiness rises from the damp of his wool jacket.

A woman walks past, wrapped in a chic raincoat. Her make-up, perfect and bright, radiates in the golden light, and her dark hair shines, swaying with every move. Above her head, she holds an umbrella. The young man wonders at her sophistication and poise. *I wish I could be her. Maybe I could slip inside her skin and disappear completely. Then no one need ever know or remember that I existed.*

His phone vibrates in his pocket.

Change of plan. Lord Moon on the Mall @ 6. C U there.

The young man reads the text twice, annoyed the plan was changed without consulting him, yet thrilled that they still remember to include him. *I wonder why they invite me at all?*

He turns back to Trafalgar Square. The rain is stopping, just spitting now, and the golden light is fading to grey. The piper is packing away. *Why isn't he cold in his sodden t-shirt and bare legs?*

Maybe he is.

What time is it? Only five fifteen. What to do? Go the pub now and be there before they arrive, everyone thinking you're desperate? Anyway, you hate drinking alone. All those people staring and wondering. You're self-conscious enough as it is. And look at yourself. You're a right state with your wet and unsuitable clothes. Idiot. Even if they don't do it out loud, they'll all be laughing at you when they see you. They'll be able to spot you're a nobody straight away, an idiot who can't even dress properly.

He looks around Trafalgar Square, wondering whether to idle some time in a gallery. *They'll be close to shutting now and, in any case, I'm not in the mood for art. What about St James's Park? I could go and see the birds.* He remembers a trip with his family when he was, what? Six? Seven? A rare trip to the capital. The pelicans jostling with the smaller birds for food under a perfect sun. It was such a long walk by the water's edge and over the bridge to the trees. Everything was so heavy in the heat. Somehow, he'd angered his Dad again.

Yes, I could walk along by the ponds and then back through Horse Guards and to the Mall. But that wouldn't take me forty-five minutes. How about walking all the way to Buckingham Palace and back again? Maybe not. Not with that split in my shoe. My feet'll be blistered by the time I get back.

I could go to a café and just sit and wait. No. I've only enough money for tonight's drinks. Maybe not enough even for that. I can't go spending it on an unnecessary coffee.

How about window shopping along St Martins and the lanes? Or a walk along the river?

Can't be bothered.

So, what then? Just stand here until it's time to go to the pub? And why did you get here so early anyway? Oh yes, that's right. You hadn't checked the forecast, had you? You'd thought you could just walk around and enjoy London. Again, not prepared.

He goes to check the time on his phone again when a hand lands on his shoulder.

– There you are.

The young man spins around to see a face staring at him.

– Oh, hi Rob. How are you?

– I'm all right. What are you doing here? I thought we were meeting at six?

Rob looks him up and down.

– Yeah, well, I thought I'd go for a walk, you know? Day off. I didn't realise it was going to rain so much.

– It pissed it down all right, didn't it? You should've checked the forecast. I did. Rob swings a folded umbrella in front of him. – I mean, how long have you been living in London now?

– Four years.

– And you still haven't worked out you should always take a brolly with you?

The young man smiled awkwardly and Rob looked him up and down again.

– Look, Neil, I've got to see a man about a dog. I'll see you in the pub at six-ish, yeah?

– Yep, see you there.

Neil watches Rob stride towards the Strand. He checks his phone. 5:30pm. Why don't you just go straight to the pub? Because you don't have the guts to push open the door without there being someone you know inside.

I wonder if anyone else feels like this? Probably not.

Still unsure of where he is going, Neil walks slowly, forlornly along the front of the National Gallery, imagining the hawkers and artists who would be crowding him out of the space if it were sunnier. The traces of chalk drawings, almost washed away by the rain, are visible in the glistening early evening light. Is that the Italian flag? Maybe not.

Talking of flags…he gazes at Canada House. What must they do inside there? That's an idea. Maybe I could move to Canada and start all over again? But how could I ever do that? Why would they take me? I have nothing, and nothing to offer.

He stares emptily at the road. A Ferrari drives past, followed closely by a bus. A cycle courier weaves in and out of the traffic and a scooter pulls up to the pavement. A woman runs across the road and disappears into a crowd waiting patiently on the other side. Who are these people? Where are they going?

A sadness sweeps over him and he thrusts his hands into his pockets. The material is cold against his legs and he shivers. He shifts on his feet and his shoes squelch.

Tomorrow is another day.

But this one isn't over yet, remember? You've still got this evening to get through. Who'll be there? Who knows. Three or four definites, the usual gang, but then everybody taking the excuse to invite along friends living on the other side of town. He shudders. All those unknown faces and awkward introductions. In any case, it'll be only men. No women. Neil sighs. Maybe, when I've had enough to drink, I can chat to a woman. Anything other than all that stupid macho conversation and the endless comparisons. Okay, fine, I'm the loser out of all of us. Can we just move on and get drunk now? Can we forget all about talking and live in that glowing half-world, where we're all together, bound by invisible wires but floating free, lost only in our own minds, adrift on the ocean?

He checks his phone again. 5:50pm. Better get it over with. I can take a slow walk around Trafalgar Square and look at the lions. What with having to wait an age at the traffic lights, there'll definitely be someone there by the time I arrive, and I won't have to deal with the pub alone.

HE CLIMBS the pub steps and pushes open the door at 6:05, but his heart sinks when he sees not one single person in the place he recognises. He panics as he glances at every face for a second and third time, examining every corner, holding on to the open door for support, wondering whether he should run away. Instead, he scuttles over to the bar and buys a pint as quickly as he can, before heading for a partially hidden spot with a view of the bar. He sips hurriedly at the cold liquid, willing the cloak of confidence to sweep through his veins and out through his skin.

By the time two of their group push through the door, he has almost finished his drink. Relieved almost beyond measure, he rushes over, asking questions and regaling them with stories before they've even taken off their coats. One offers to buy Neil a pint, and Neil makes a note to buy a round in return at the earliest opportunity so he can spend the absolute minimum. If I time it right, I might get away with having to buy only three or four drinks in total.

The three men toast each other and quickly finish their pints. Another friend arrives and Neil offers to buy a round, happy to fulfil his duties for the evening, but is dismayed when it's suggested they get whisky chasers. But I can't say no. We're forged in complicity and drunkenness is our goal. No, I cannot say no. He checks over his shoulder that no others have arrived to add to his bill.

Eventually, it is done. His money is spent and four pints and four whiskies stand on the bar. The friend who suggested the chasers pours a whisky into each pint.

– It gets you drunk faster, he says, grinning mischievously. – That concentration of alcohol in a pint, it's perfect for getting you hammered. It's been scientifically proven.

– Okay, well, here's to drunkenness, Neil says, grabbing his pint and raising it in a toast.

Now I can slip away from the world and into my drunken cocoon.

They each drink down their pints in determined silence, slamming down their glasses onto the bar one after another.

– Who's next, the grinning friend asks.

And so they launch into pint after pint, chaser after chaser. The group grows with each new face, until it splinters into an endless flow of factions formed, disbanded, reformed, periodically uniting as one to raise a toast, before splitting again to talk more and more insistently, more and more incoherently.

Neil looks away from their noisy, glowing, self-contained world of alcoholic complicity and in-jokes. The rest of the pub is over-lit and sharp, an angular trap for those that stray from their pack. Couples and families sitting quietly at tables, old men standing on their own, Japanese tourists and a couple of actors from the theatre next door. Neil drifts between the two worlds, not wanting to be in the maelstrom of his friends but alienated from the genteel pub. We are the ones out of place. How did we end up here, of all places?

– How did we end up here, of all places, he asks Pete, a shy younger member of their group.

– What did you say?

– Why did we come here tonight, to this pub?

– Um, I don't know. Weren't we always coming here?

– No, we were supposed to go the All Bar One near Charing Cross.

– Oh. Don't you like it here?

– It's not that. I just wondered why we came here instead.

– Dunno.

Neil turns to Rob, who is heading to the toilet.

– Hey Rob, why did we end up here tonight?

– Dan used to work here. He wanted to see his old colleagues.

– Okay. Fair enough. Where's Dan? I haven't seen him yet.

– He's not coming.

– Why not?

– He can't make it.

Rob pushes his way to the toilet. Neil wonders why it was Dan's choice. He knows he couldn't have coped with the responsibility, but a sliver of jealousy slices through him all the same.

He glances around the bar, wondering if he could leave and anyone would notice. He hears the music for the first time. It seems loud and insistent, and his mind bristles against the agitated rhythm. How could I have not heard it before? Another drink. That is the only answer.

As if by magic, a pint appears. He contemplates the acid

yellow liquid, watching the bubbles slide up the glass. Down in one, someone says. Who was that? He doesn't care. Down it goes, all gone, save a bolt of coldness through him and the rasp of the bubbles against his throat.

Another. This one's a shot of Sambuca. Oh, it's going to be one of those evenings. He catches a friend's eye, whose name he has forgotten. He winks at Neil. Conspiratorially? Patronisingly? What other ways are there? Whatever, Neil feels a hot flush of pleasure at someone wanting to include him. But then a pang of doubt. What if he is patronising me after all? What if he thinks I'm just a kid, out of place among men? Men have always winked at me. Why? He shudders and turns away.

Oh, I still haven't drunk the shot. He glances around. I'm almost the last. He quickly brings the small, thick glass to his lips and stares down at the shivering black liquid. His stomach tightens. Don't be sick now. He tips the glass and swallows it down, the sticky, sugary, burnt-tasting liquid sliding down inside him, an alcoholic oil slick coating his insides. The winking man is staring at Neil, smiling to himself. He is laughing at me, I know it.

– It's the closest thing to coke that's legal, someone shouts in his ear.

I thought that was tequila, Neil thinks, but he says nothing and simply smiles.

– It's brilliant, the voice adds, I always pull when I've had Sambuca. Makes me confident.

– Yeah, Neil says, nodding his head. He definitely means tequila.

Slowly at first, and then faster and faster, the evening spins out of control, a car sliding on black ice in slow motion. Time stops in the over-lit pub and then accelerates, pushing them into a separate universe. Neil becomes aware of himself, spilling a pint he doesn't remember being given over his shoes and the hem of his jacket. He glances around again. Those other people. He had forgotten them. Now, in their separate universe, he has forgotten leaving, forgotten doubt and forgotten paranoia, forgotten himself. I'm free to be myself. Is that it? No. I'm free to simply act and react, without thinking. Why can't I be like this when I'm sober? I want to stay like this forever, this bulletproof me, this armour-clad, sleek, shiny, superior version of me. Neil the Joke Slayer, Neil the All-Seeing Comprehender, Neil the Smart-Talking Smooth Operator. Neil the Playboy, the Ladykiller. I can play now in the Kingdom of Men, stand tall among these masculine, confident Men, and feel as if I belong. Who am I now? I am Neil, a Man. A real Man, and I am one of Them.

XII

A TAP ON HIS SHOULDER. NEIL TURNS TO SEE THE BARMAN standing next to him, anger filling his unshaven, doughy face.

– Do you know him?

– Who, Neil asks, noting the drunken slip in his voice.

– Him.

The barman points to the floor. There, prostate, unconscious, almost peaceful on the stained floor, lies Dave's large, overweight frame, perfectly arranged in the symmetrical design of the carpet.

– Yes, I do.

– Well, you need to sort him out and get him out of here because I don't want him dying on my carpet.

– Right. Of course.

Neil looks around the group, who have stepped back and stare at him with worry in their eyes, their shared universe closed off forever.

– Right, Neil says to himself.

The barman heads back to the bar but Neil grabs his arm. The barman looks down at Neil's hand.

– Can you call an ambulance? I'll get him up and outside.

The barman nods and walks away. Neil looks around the group again. Why don't they do anything? Why me? Why me? Why the fuck don't they do anything? Why is it left to me? He looks down at Dave. No problem, he thinks. I am Neil the Capable, Neil the Responsible. I can handle it.

– No problem, he says out loud.

He points at one of their number.

– It's John, right?

The young man nods.

– Give me a hand to get him up.

John steps forward, unsure what to do, his hands tucked into his armpits. Neil bends down to check Dave's breathing but falls onto his hands and knees. Concentrate, you prick. Concentrate. Neil leans into Dave and his head sways as he tries to catch the sound of his breathing. He can barely hear anything in the cacophony of the pub. He checks Dave's pulse. Very weak. Neil's stomach turns. Oh, God, he could die. This is real. He looks up at the group, who see the fear in his eyes.

– Is he okay?

– He'll be fine. We just need to get him some fresh air.

– Are you sure, asks John, his hands still in his armpits.

Neil nods and puts his hands under Dave's arms and tries to pull him up. The drunken deadweight is heavier than Neil expected and he struggles until John finally pulls his hands out of his armpits and gives him a hand. Slowly, awkwardly they drag Dave upright and onto its feet.

– Let's take him outside while we wait for the ambulance.

– Okay, John says, trying to catch his breath.

They stumble across the bar, the other customers backing out of their way and clearing tables and chairs from their path. They reach the steps down to the street, the door held open by a grey-haired man with a frightened expression. The cold air stirs the sleeping beast. As the two smaller men half push, half pull Dave down the steps, the beast lashes out, catching Neil full in the face. The three of them fall head-first down the steps, Dave landing on the back of his head and Neil banging his forehead on the hard concrete slabs. His head spinning, Neil springs to his feet and checks Dave. But the pool of blood is already forming around Dave's hair and Neil's heart sinks. Dazed, John sits up and stares aghast at the slick of blood, dark and thick, that continues to grow and pool around the fallen man's skull, filling the gaps between the paving stones.

– Oh no, Neil says, the tears welling up.

– We'll take it from here, says a rough voice with a South London accent, and Neil is pushed aside by two paramedics. Neil steps back and smiles at John in relief before an intense, throbbing ache pulses across his forehead and he doubles up with the pain. By the time Neil opens his eyes again, the paramedics have bandaged Dave's wound and are loading him into the ambulance.

– Can I come with him, Neil asks timidly, holding his forehead.

– No, you'll have to make your own way.

– Where are you going?

– St Thomas's.

– Okay, Neil says to the slamming ambulance door.

Imaging himself in a US cop show, he pats the side of the ambulance as it drives away, relieved. But the retreating van reveals Pete, with a sheepish look on his face and his hand aloft, a thick stream of bright red blood pouring down his arm.

– What the fuck happened to you, Neil asks incredulously.

– I cut myself.

– I can see that. How?

– I fell over. I was holding a bottle of gin, and the top broke off when I hit the floor and it sliced through my finger.

– What the fuck, Neil says, wincing. – Has it cut through all the way?

– No, but it's bad.

– Why didn't you go in the ambulance?

– They wouldn't take me.

– What? Why?

– They said I should get a taxi.

– With that? Who the fuck is going to take us with you like that? You'll get blood everywhere.

– I know. The young man looked down at the floor, crestfallen. – Do you think I'll lose my finger?

– No, no, you won't. Just hold on, okay? Neil turns to John. – Look, can you run inside and get us a load of kitchen roll? The more the better.

– Yep.

John bounds up the steps two-by-two and runs into the bar.

– I suppose I'd better get on with hailing a taxi.

Pete gives an embarrassed smile, trying to hold back the tears. Neil moves towards the edge of the pavement but then stops himself.

– Where did you get a bottle of gin from?

– It was in my jacket. I was topping up my drinks with it.

Neil shakes his head and rubs his eyes, aware once more of the dull ache pulsing through his forehead. John appears from inside the pub with a wad of kitchen roll. Neil looks down the road but steps back as a red bus roars past his face. He spots a taxi and glances at Pete, his hand a candy floss of kitchen roll.

– Are you ready?

– Yep.

Neil hails the cab and it slows to a stop beside him. Pete

steps forward, an apologetic look on his face, as Neil sticks his head through the window.

– St Thomas's Hospital, please.

– Okay, jump in.

Once they're settled in, the cab turns back up Whitehall and down Northumberland Avenue towards the Thames.

– So what happened to you then, the driver asks via the rear-view mirror.

– I fell with a bottle of gin in my hand. It cut straight through my finger.

– What are the chances of that, eh?

– Yeah, Pete says sadly.

– Don't worry, we'll be at St Thomas's in no time.

Neil stares at the endless stream of people out for the evening, heading to what? A pub for drinks with their friends? A romantic dinner? A show? No, it's too late for that. A young woman with bleach-blond hair in a tight shiny dress walks hand in hand with a tall man in a checked shirt with gelled-down hair. The woman laughs as they walk up towards Trafalgar Square. A pang of jealousy pierces Neil.

A scooter weaves in between the traffic. The taxi slows as they reach the traffic lights. In front is the Thames and the Hispaniola. Neil thinks back to an evening on the boat two years before. He remembers being very drunk and nearly dropping his phone overboard, and the sense of not belonging in the crowd of well-dressed and confident people. What was the occasion? Can't remember. But he does remember the vicious argument afterwards with his girlfriend and shudders.

The lights change and the taxi lurches forward. Neil looks down at his hands. He is drifting in and out of consciousness. The taxi is loud and insistent. He looks up, but the lights on Victoria Embankment are bright and piercing and he returns to inspecting his hands. Is there something wrong with them? They seem…full? He flexes his fingers and tries to gather himself. He remembers Pete and turns to speak, but Pete is staring out the window, his bandaged hand resting against the top of the door. The driver checks his passengers in the rear-view mirror.

– They're building a giant Ferris wheel over there.

– Oh yes? Where, Neil asks, trying to pull himself together.

– On the other side, by the old GLC building. Like the one in Vienna, but bigger.

– Oh right, okay. When will that be?

Neil focuses on the seat in front of him and listens intently to the driver.

– They said it should be ready before the end of the year, by the millennium. They reckon you'll be able to see right across London.

– If it's not cloudy.

– Exactly, the cab driver says, laughing.

The car slows at the end of Victoria Embankment and, as it turns onto Westminster Bridge, Neil stares up at Big Ben before it's quickly lost from view and they drive up and over the bridge, gliding down to the hospital.

– Nearly there, Neil says quietly to Pete.

– Hmm.

When they arrive at the emergency entrance, Pete wanders inside while Neil pays for the cab from a fiver he found in his pocket. He hangs back for a moment and stares up at the building and the cloudy night sky.

Inside, Neil searches for Pete but cannot see him in the waiting room or the corridors. An overwhelming tiredness sweeps over him and the throbbing ache returns, weighing him down. Sit down, lie down, anywhere, on anything. But I need to piss first. He heads for the toilets, stumbling as he walks. A doctor is walking towards him and stops, watching him.

– Are you okay?

– What? Um, yes, I'm fine. Thank you.

– Are you sure?

– Yes, yes, I'm okay.

Neil pushes through the toilet doors and disappears inside.

XIII

THE DOCTOR WATCHES THE DOOR SWING SHUT AND FROWNS, then walks on down the corridor. Where was I going? She searches through the foggy recesses of her mind. Oh yes, to get coffee. What was it? Two espressos, a latte, one americano and whatever I want. She walks on in a daze, barely registering the elderly woman lying on a trolley, panic in her eyes.

– Nurse?

The doctor walks on.

– Nurse?

The doctor stops and turns.

– I'm not a nurse.

– Sorry love. Do you know when the doctor will come and see me?

– I am a doctor.

– But the man, the one I saw before.

She sighs and walks over to the woman.

– How long have you been here?

– I don't know. Several hours, I think. I fell asleep. What's happening?

The doctor looks at the sheaf of papers tucked in the tray at the end of the trolley.

– You came in at nine, is that right?

– I think so.

– It says you're waiting for a test, to check to your heart. No one has come to do that?

– No doctor, not yet.

– Okay, I'll look into it. You just hold tight and someone will be over soon. Do you want a glass of water? To go to the toilet?

– A glass of water would be nice, thank you.

– I'll get the nurse to come and see you. You wait here and everything will be sorted out. Okay?

– Yes doctor. Thank you doctor.

She wanders on down the corridor, pushing through the double doors and into the strip-lit, low-key hubbub of A&E. A nurse walks past her towards the nursing station. The doctor catches her eye and points to the corridor.

– There's a woman out there.

– Sorry, I'm going for my break...

– Before you go for your break, there's a woman out there...

– Okay, the nurse says impatiently.

– ...who's been waiting on a trolley for an ECG since nine pm. I make that nearly three hours. So before you go on your break, can you quickly check what's happening with her ECG, and take her a glass of water? She's parched. Okay?

– Okay doctor.

– Thank you.

She continues through A&E, trying not to catch anyone else's eye and hoping they end up having a quiet night. What is it? Friday? Fat chance of that. And the time? Almost midnight? Things should start hotting up soon.

On her way back, laden with coffees, she takes another

route, through the now-quiet outpatient clinics, a little forbidding in their functional coldness at this time of night, to the staff lifts.

Back on the surgical ward, she runs through her patients in her head as she goes to the doctors room, working out which operations she can assist on. She sighs. All this constant fighting over patients just to get enough experience. Is it all worth it?

She heads into the staffroom. Three doctors lounging across standard-issue NHS armchairs pull themselves up when they see her.

– Hi Jen, one says. – Thanks for going. Did you remember everything this time?

– Yes, I think so. Two espressos, a latte and an americano. That's it, right?

– Yep, but what did you get for yourself?

Jen looks down at the four coffees and her face falls.

– Oh, no. I forgot. I was concentrating so much on remembering what you wanted that I forgot all about me.

– And that's why you're such a great doctor, says one of the others, grabbing the latte.

– Lucky for you, says another, taking one of the espressos. – Matt has gone into surgery and won't be back for hours, so you can have his.

– There you go, some divine justice for you, says the third.

Jen smiles and, taking the remaining espresso, slumps into one of the armchairs.

– Anything happen while I was away?

– No, nothing. All quiet on the Western Front.

– The calm before the storm.

Jen glances down at the magazine she started reading three days ago but still hasn't finished. I can't be bothered to read that now.

– How's your exam prep going, she asks the others.

Before they can respond, a nurse sticks her head around the door.

– We've just had someone sent up from A&E, can one of you…?

– I'll go, Jen says, pulling herself out of her armchair.

The nurse disappears and Jen shuffles after her, sipping her coffee.

– Good luck, one of the other doctors calls after her.

Jen ambles after the nurse, her mind drifting. When she pushes through the curtain, the patient, who is sat uncomfortably on the bed, stares straight at the nurse.

– I thought you said you'd bring the doctor.

– I did. This is the doctor.

He looks at Jen with a mix of anger and fear.

– What do you mean? Can't I get a proper doctor?

Jen sighs.

– I am a proper doctor. Now, if you wouldn't mind lying back…

– But nurse, nurse.

– What is it?

– I don't want to be seen by one of 'them'.

The patient jerks his head at Jen and the nurse looks at Jen's placid expression, wondering how she manages to stay calm.

– I'm so sorry, doctor, the nurse says.

– Could you please just lay back so I can inspect your leg, Jen asks with no trace of emotion in her voice.

The patient stares at Jen, fear in his eyes, then complies.

HOURS LATER, Jen calls the staff lift and listens to the machinery pulling it up from the ground floor. She tilts her head from side to side and feels her vertebrae click. She rubs her right shoulder and rotates her arm. Maybe Steve will give me a massage tonight. What time is it? Four am. Already? He'll be asleep. Maybe tomorrow.

Downstairs, she wanders back towards A&E. As she turns into the corridor, she sees the old woman, still on the trolley but lying still. With a turn of her stomach, she wonders if the woman is all right. She steps over and checks her breathing. Shallow but okay. Jen reads her notes and the ECG report. The woman has already been discharged and can go home.

Jen pushes through the double doors and stops the first nurse that passes her.

– What is that woman still doing here?

– Sorry, doctor. What woman?

– The one asleep on the trolley out there. Jen points towards the double doors. – She was discharged hours ago. Why is she still here?

The nurse thinks for a moment.

– Oh yes. Annie. She needs to be discharged to a nursing home as she can't look after herself. But there's no places available and, in any case, the local ambulance doesn't operate at this time of night.

– Why don't we just put her on a ward for the night, on a proper bed, rather than leaving her out there in that freezing corridor?

– She's not ill enough and anyway, without any nursing-home places, she could end up blocking a bed for ages.

Jen sighs. – And what about her family?

– They live too far away and don't have any room, apparently.

Jen shakes her head. – Okay, I get it. Thanks.

– Sorry doctor, but there's not much we can do right now to help her.

– I know, I know. Just keep an eye on her, okay?

– Yes, of course.

Jen wanders across A&E and out into the receding night. She crosses Westminster Bridge Road and glances at Parliament and Big Ben as she crosses onto York Road. Light gathers at the edges of the sky.

> *...tomorrow, when the dawn*
> *On saffron wheels leads on another day,*
> *We'll start our work again.*

Jen shakes her head, trying not to let the hurt and pain seep in. Fatigue sweeps over her and she shudders.

As she trudges on towards Waterloo, she becomes aware of footsteps just behind her. She instinctively braces herself and slows down to let whoever it is pass. She glances at the dishevelled young man stumbling past her. I'm sure I've seen him before. The young man walks on, and she notices his untied shoelaces. No, can't place him.

XIV

Neil, drunk and lost in so many thoughts, half-walks, half-stumbles along York Road.

That woman just now. I've seen her. Somewhere. You could turn back and have a look. No, don't do that, you might fall over. But where? Where did you see her? Where have you been? There must have been somewhere in-between...start from the beginning. Well, not right at the beginning, that would take ages, but from the taxi. So, where? Where did I go? I lost Pete when I paid for the cab, taxi, whatever. So yes, then I was walking through A&E. My head hurt, my head hurt a lot. Does it still? Ouch, yes, that's sore. Oh, I hope it's not serious. Forget about it, you can't do anything about it now, now you're on your way home. But where did Pete go? Where could he have got to? And what about Dave? Shit, shit, Dave. What happened to h... Maybe you've had a text or something? Hold on...Just pull the damn phone out your pock...stuck in there, again....There you go. No, nothing. Hope he's okay. Hope he's not dead. Or disabled. In a wheelchair, unable to walk and look after himself. Oh God, and I forgot all about him. Oh no. And

Pete. I didn't even try...But wait a minute. What did I do, exactly? Where did I go? I must have gone...That's it. I went to the toilet in the hospital, when I couldn't find Pete. But what happened then? Oh yes, I fell asleep, with my trousers round my ankles and my head lolling like a puppet. I woke up with that cleaner banging on the cubicle door. What was it? An hour? I must have been asleep for at least an hour. Easily. My legs were so cold and stiff, and I was so tired pulling up my trousers. But what did I do after that? I must've done something. What time is it now? Four am or something? What the hell have I been doing since midnight? Think, man, think. There's only so many options. I can remember walking...I'm walking now, one foot in front of the other, step, step, step. Look at the tarmac, all little grey stones and so much crap. All that chewing gum and the dirt from the buses and taxis. Especially here, by Waterloo station. I wonder what it tastes like? What would it be like to get down on your hands and knees and lick the tarmac? Like the Pope. He's always kissing the floor, bending down when he gets out of a plane. He knows what tarmac tastes like. But I bet he doesn't lick it, though. Just a peck. Maybe he doesn't let his lips touch the floor at all, just says he did. Yep, I definitely kissed it. Yep, just like last time. Funny, this tarmac reminds me of some just like it in South America. Or maybe he doesn't speak like that. Oh, a bus. At this time? A night bus. Going where? Elephant. what the odds are of a night bus to Elephant passing me exactly then? Hey, that's it. I remember now. I went to a bar. I left...no, I don't remember that. I don't remember leaving the hospital. But I...remember...yes, I remember walking down towards Lambeth North. I saw the Tube station. And it's not far, right? I was looking for somewhere. I must have been looking for a bar. Did I find one? Oh, hold on, forget that for a minute and think about now. Where shall I go? I could go down here and cross on

Hungerford Bridge or walk on and cross at Waterloo. Steps now or steps later? Steps now. Anyway, it's nicer this way, along by the arches and up to the Royal Festival Hall. What the hell? My damn jacket won't sit straight again. Just get it onto one shoulder and then the other...well, it's not suddenly going to stop being cheap shit because I ask it to. Oh bollocks, did I put my keys in that pocket again? You know the lining's ripped, you dick, but you always forget and put them in there anyway. Yep, exactly like last time, they've gone into the lining of the jacket. Well done, idiot, well bloody done. Always the same, eh? Now you've got to go fishing around until you can work them back through the hole and into the pocket. Damned idiot. Ooh, nice woman. Shiny, like...oh, wow, look at her. She's hot. Those shiny, tight trousers. Sexy. And look at her tight jacket and her hair. Wow, she's amazing. Where's she going? Where has she been? I would love to...no, don't glance at me, it's not worth it. You're way out of my league and...that's it. That's where I was. I was in that little bar I went to with Dave that time. In the backstreets behind the Tube station. That's where I must've gone after the hospital. I didn't know it was open so late. Oh yes, that taste in my mouth, I must've had beer. Quite a bit. But did I vomit? I don't remember, but it tastes like I did. Let's just check my clothes. No, no signs of vomit. Maybe I just retched and I still have the taste? Yes, that's it, after the second beer, I think I had a shot of something. Oh yes, it was disgusting and I retched afterwards. I must've had that third pint afterwards to get rid of the taste. I didn't need it though. And, ugh, I can still feel the cold crawling up my face after that one. Oh here we are, up the steps, now....Did I go to the toilets after that drink? Ah yes, I did. The lights in there were horrible. And all that graffiti. Still, the piss was one of the best I've ever...Oh, the stairs up to the bridge. Christ, they're difficult. Did they have to make them so steep? Pffff, it's you, you prick. You shouldn't drink so much. You need to start running again, boy. *You should cut down on your pork life mate / Get some exercise.* You are not fit at all. Ah, yes, that's better at the top. Jesus, the fire in my thighs is incredible. All that lactic acid. How you have fallen from your past glories, my friend. But you're here now, on the bridge to the other side, to the bright lights of the West End, and to home. Eventually. Christ, you have so much further to walk. Maybe an hour. You're going to be dead by the time you get there, especially with that bloody split in your shoe. Can't be helped, though. You just have to push on, like an Antarctic explorer. No, not that. Scott of the Sahara! That's him. Oh shit, I need a piss. Really badly. Maybe further along the bridge, that dark bit at the end where it connects to Charing Cross. It always smells like everyone pisses there. Seriously, are you going to walk all the way home? No choice, mate. You definitely can't afford a taxi. You could take a night bus. No, all that swaying, neon lights and other people. No, it's better to walk home. It is your destiny, my boy. You must stuffer the pain and the tiredness, for it is your destiny to traverse London in the dark. Think of De Quincey. He walked all the way to London. Poor kid, just missing her like that. How sad. The water does look dark and heavy, doesn't it? Like molten rock. Place your hands on the rail, in case you fall. You could fall, couldn't you? You could 'fall', and then it would be all over. All that struggle would be over, wouldn't it. And life would, well, be over. Yes. That is a nice idea. The Savoy looks nice at night, doesn't it, and Somerset House. And look at St Paul's, nestled there in the distance. What a beautiful sweep as the river turns. The Royal Festival Hall is always so much bigger than I remember. Is it ugly? You used to think so, didn't you? When you saw Tony Blair giving his speech at dawn, after the election. But now it seems...I don't know. It's there, part of the family.

It's like trying to objectively scrutinise an aunt. It doesn't work. Are those barges always there? Or do they move? Maybe. But why would they move? And what do they do? Collect rubbish from the river? It's quiet tonight, isn't it? Not so many people. The boats are empty and shut, and the Tube station. Embankment. What's that, down there? It looks like a bar, or maybe a club. I haven't seen it before. Maybe it's new. I could go. I think I have enough money on my card. Oh, no, they'd want an entrance fee at this time, and I don't have any cash. If I take some out, my card won't work, and then how will I pay for food this week? It's still five days to payday. How can it always be like this? How can it always end up like this? It's so ridiculous and awful and you're such a...gosh, that red is so beautiful coming across the sky. Of course, it's dawn. *Rosy-fingered dawn.* Nearly daytime already. So beautiful. London, you are beautiful like this. Look at yourself. And there's so much out there. You can be anything here. Forget no money and your shit clothes and your tiredness. This is the place you have to be, and you will be okay one day, my friend. One day you will be more than okay. You will reach your destiny and have glory. You shall triumph... Although right now you need a piss. Maybe in that corner. There's no one coming.

THE LAKE

I

THE SOLDIER'S FEET KICK UP SMALL STONES AND DUST AS HE IS
dragged across the hot ground. His head hangs limp between
his shoulders, and barely a trace of pain registers on his face
as he is pulled along.

Eventually, he is dumped behind a truck in the shade. He
winces at the pain slicing him in two as he lands. He hangs
his head and lets his arms fall by his side, unable to do
anything more. A man in the same uniform but with a
straggly beard kneels down beside him.

– Just hold on, Hans.

– Mmm…

– Hans, can you hear me? Eh?

– Uh, yes.

– The helicopter is on its way. It should be here in…The
man checks his watch…Ten minutes. Max.

– Mmm…

– Did you hear me? Hey, Hans.

The bearded man gently slaps Hans, adding yellow dust
to the sweat pouring down the young soldier's face.

– Yes, yes. I heard you.

Hans slowly opens his eyes and looks up into the bearded man's face.

– Thank you for saving me, Carl, he says weakly. – What happened?

– An IED.

Hans frowns and fear flashes across his face.

– My legs...?

– I don't know, Hans. Just wait for the helicopter and let the docs do their work.

– I can't feel them.

– I know, but there's nothing we can do now. Just wait and let them take a proper look at you.

Hans looks out into the heat haze. Everything is hot and yellow. He turns some soil over in his hands.

– The others?

– I don't know. You were hanging out of the side, so I dragged you out first, but by the time I got back it was too hot for me to get close.

A tear rolls down Hans' cheek.

– They trusted me.

– Don't think about it, Hans. They knew what they were doing.

Hans swallows and searches Carl's face.

– Did they?

Carl stares back at him.

– Look, I'm sorry, Hans, but I have to go. I have to see if there are any other survivors. Can you wait here and keep calm until the helicopter comes? It's on its way. It should be vey soon. Okay?

– Okay.

– You'll be okay. Just hang on.

Carl squeezes Hans' shoulder and stands up. Hans watches him glance from side to side and then run back the way they came.

Hans swallows and tries to resign himself to waiting. He watches an insect scramble over a rock and then run under the truck. The heat is rising and he wishes he could drag himself to a better spot to wait. In the distance, there is an explosion.

II

In the dark green forest, the birds arc and turn through the dappled light, following the line of the brook as it wends its way down the valley. A large white butterfly dances past the soldier and lands on a flower. He breathes deep the cool, clear air, and smiles.

– Wait for me.

He turns and watches her step down from a fallen tree trunk, a bunch of flowers in her hand, and run towards him.

He sees, here in this green kingdom and away from the grinding noise of the city, how she is borne of nature, a lithe and athletic creature that radiates grace. His heart leaps for her and wishes they could stay here forever, building a house in the woods and leaving the world far behind.

She stops right in front of him, panting slightly, and smiles, her soft dusting of freckles moving as she does so. If only he could melt into her and they become one.

– I love you.

– I love you too.

He turns and they walk together along the brook hand-in-hand. Eventually, they reach a clearing, a perfect circle between the trees where the brook pools and turns. The lights catches the purple and yellow flowers as they dance in the breeze, and dragonflies flit back and forth over the surface of the water.

THE PAIN RIPS THROUGH HANS' body and he wakes, surprised to find himself in the heat and the dust. The sun seems hotter now, and he wonders if he can drag himself further into the shade. He pushes against the dust and rocks, his uniform catching and scraping with every millimetre. He is no longer horrified to see his immobile legs, which slide like a doll's within the material of his trousers. Now he is just curious. Puzzled even.

Eventually, he manages to pull his body further under the shade of the truck and falls back, sweating profusely, against one of the tyres.

A soldier runs in front of him and is blown up. Panicking, Hans listens intently for the helicopter, but cannot hear it.

Everything falls quiet. There is no shouting anymore, no more gunfire.

III

THE SOLDIER STEPS OUT OF THE VINTAGE CAR AND STARES AT the large mansion. He does not know how he got there or where he is, yet the house seems familiar. There is something about the sweep of the gravel drive, the statues nestling in the floral borders, and the faux crenelations on the rooftop that reassure him he is in the right place.

He walks up the stone steps to the double front door, which is open, and walks in. An older man, in a tailcoat and bowtie, is waiting for him, smiling. He shakes the soldier's hand firmly and seems to suggest he likes the way he is dressed. The soldier looks down and realises he is wearing his dress uniform. Why? Why am I wearing that?

By the time he looks up again, the footman has gone and there are people running around with flower arrangements and table decorations, bundles of streamers and bottles of champagne. The soldier smiles involuntarily.

He walks through the house and stops to gaze out over the vast garden, one side of which is filled with marquees and smaller tents. All sorts of people, some he recognises, are getting ready for something. Trays laden with food and drinks pass, and a small orchestra is rehearsing. The table decorations he saw earlier are being carefully put into place. What is this all for? A wedding? For whom?

The soldier spots a path that leads down to the forest at the end of the garden. He steps onto the soft, comforting grass and a light rain begins to fall, a gentle, caressing fine mist that coats everything it touches.

The soldier walks past the brightly coloured marquees and the waiters and footmen running back and forth. No-one notices him as he passes, and he walks on towards the forest, everything falling away as he crosses into the dark shade of the trees. Every leaf, every branch, every flower is dripping. The enveloping moisture becomes rain. He raises his hands and watches the soft drops land on his skin.

He looks up and sees through the raindrops something glowing in the distance. He steps over tree roots and pushes back the sodden branches as makes his way into the interior of the forest. The ground is soft beneath his feet, yielding, like moss. On and on he walks, the rain falling more and more heavily, while the distant glow becomes ever-stronger.

Eventually, he reaches a clearing, a perfect circle between the trees, and stops. The light falls through the raindrops from all directions, creating rainbows wherever he looks. Once his eyes adjust, he sees a woman in a white dress near the middle of the clearing. She stands in front of a small pond surrounded by flowers, where dragonflies flit back and forth over the surface of the water.

She turns and smiles and he feels the electricity flow through him. She radiates grace and beauty. It is her.

He approaches and she stretches out her hand to meet his. The rain falls faster now, in large, heavy drops, and the pond grows and widens into a lake, covering the ground and advancing closer and closer to the woman's feet. He looks down and sees a dark red stain growing on his uniform. His legs become weak and he realises he is running out of time.

He stretches out his hand and she pulls him alongside her. He knows he is safe now, and they stand in the teeming rain, contemplating the lake growing by their feet. He looks at her. She is perfect, radiant, glowing in the light refracted by the raindrops.

The drops become larger and larger, and they drum rhythmically on the surface of the lake and the leaves of the trees. The soldier and the woman, hand-in-hand, stare at the surface of the water and then slowly walk towards it. The water laps against their feet and they wade on and on, the dark water higher and higher, creeping up their bodies until their heads disappear beneath the surface.

They swim now, into the infinite darkness, hand-in-hand, further and further from the light. In the clearing, the rain drums against the surface of the water, the light catching the drops and the wings of the dragonflies that flit back and forth.

A LOCAL TRIBESMAN squats on his haunches in the shadow of the truck and contemplates the face of the young soldier. He seems peaceful, asleep even. Or he would if his unseeing eyes were not open.

The tribesman sighs and closes the young man's eyes before straightening up and walking away.

ABOUT THE AUTHOR

L.A. Davenport was born in Cork, Ireland, in 1973. He graduated from Emmanuel College, Cambridge, in Medical Sciences and Archeology and Anthropology in 1996. He has written several novels, numerous short stories and novellas, and countless articles and essays. He divides his time between Lincolnshire and the Côte d'Azur. Among other things, he likes long walks, typewriters and big cups of tea.

To find out when L.A. Davenport has a new book out, and get the latest updates, visit his official website at Pushing the Wave.

BY L.A. DAVENPORT

FICTION

Escape, The Hunter Cut

The Nucleus of Reality, or the Recollections of Thomas P—

Escape

Dear Lucifer and Other Stories

The Marching Band Emporium

NON-FICTION

Pushing the Wave 2023

Pushing the Wave 2017–2022

More Life as a Dog

My Life as a Dog

P-WAVE PRESS

Thank you for reading!

We hope you enjoyed this book. At P-Wave Press, we're passionate about unique and thought-provoking stories.

Scan the QR code below to:

- Explore all our books
- See upcoming titles
- Share your comments and book reviews
- Order any P-Wave Press book

We'd love to hear from you at p-wavepress.co.uk.